Claudia Gets Her Guy

Other books by Ann M. Martin

P.S. Longer Letter Later
(written with Paula Danziger)
Leo the Magnificat
Rachel Parker, Kindergarten Show-off
Eleven Kids, One Summer
Ma and Pa Dracula
Yours Turly, Shirley
Ten Kids, No Pets
Slam Book
Just a Summer Romance
Missing Since Monday
With You and Without You
Me and Katie (the Pest)
Stage Fright
Inside Out
Bummer Summer

THE KIDS IN MS. COLMAN'S CLASS series
BABY-SITTERS LITTLE SISTER series
THE BABY-SITTERS CLUB mysteries
THE BABY-SITTERS CLUB series
CALIFORNIA DIARIES series

Claudia Gets Her Guy

Ann M. Martin

AN
APPLE
PAPERBACK

SCHOLASTIC INC.
New York Toronto London Auckland Sydney
Mexico City New Delhi Hong Kong

ISBN 0-590-52338-4

12 11 10 9 8 7 6 5 4 3 2 1 0 1 2 3 4 5/0

Printed in the U.S.A. 40

First Scholastic printing, February 2000

The author gratefully acknowledges
Ellen Miles
for her help in
preparing this manuscript.

Special thanks
to the helpful staff at
Central Vermont Adult Basic
Education for their
expertise.

Claudia Gets Her Guy

Chapter 1

"Aaahhh! Peace at last!" With a huge sigh of relief, I flung myself down on the couch. It was nearly ten, and I had finally, *finally* managed to tuck all three Rodowsky boys into their beds. With any luck, the rest of my Saturday night would be quiet and relaxing.

THUMP! CRASH!

I glanced toward the ceiling. The noises had come from upstairs. Not a good sign. I held my breath and crossed my fingers.

"Claudia!"

Jackie's voice. Big surprise.

I rolled off the couch and stood up. "Coming!" I called, trying to sound cheerful and patient, like the professional baby-sitter I am.

I ran up the stairs. Jackie, who's seven, was walking down the hall toward me. That was the good news — he could still walk. The bad news? He was rubbing his elbow.

"What is it?" I asked.

"I fell out of bed," Jackie answered, sniffing a little. His red hair was tousled, his freckles stood out against his pale skin, and he looked unbelievably cute in his black-and-white-plaid flannel pj's. "I think I broke my funny bone."

I nodded seriously. I didn't know if the funny bone was breakable, but if it was, Jackie would be the kid to break his. He is the most accident-prone child I've ever met. My friends and I, who belong to the Baby-sitters Club, or BSC, have a nickname for Jackie. We call him the Walking Disaster.

"Let's take a look," I said, kneeling down next to Jackie. I had a feeling — call it baby-sitter's intuition — that he was probably okay. I knew he'd had a bad bump, but if he had really broken something I figured he'd be screaming in pain. Carefully, I pushed up his pajama sleeve and inspected the elbow. I didn't see any swelling or bruising. "Can you move it?" I asked.

Tentatively, Jackie moved his arm. "Uh-huh," he said.

I put on a very serious look. "In that case, I don't

think we'll have to perform a funny-bone transplant," I said.

Jackie cracked up.

"What happened?" Shea, Jackie's older brother (he's nine), rubbed his eyes as he walked down the hall toward us.

"Jackie fell out of bed, but he's okay," I said, standing up and putting my hands on Jackie's shoulders. I steered him toward his room. "Time for everybody to get back into bed."

I tucked Jackie in again, made sure Shea was settled, and lowered the dimmer switch on the hall lights. I was heading down the stairs when I heard a little voice call my name.

"Claudia?"

It was Archie, the youngest Rodowsky boy. He's four.

I sighed. "What is it?"

"I'm thirsty."

"Okay," I called, turning away from the stairs. "Stay in bed, and I'll bring you a glass of water."

A few minutes later, I plopped down on the couch again. Before I relaxed totally, I listened for noises from upstairs.

Not a peep.

"Aaahh," I said, leaning back. It's funny. I love

baby-sitting, mostly because I love hanging out with kids. But I also like this part, the time when the kids are in bed and I have a chance to relax. It's always fun to hang out on another family's couch, read their magazines, and check out the contents of their fridge (if you have permission, that is).

The Rodowskys have a very nice couch (it's covered in old, worn brown leather), excellent magazines (*Vogue*, *Glamour*, and *People*, to name a few), and awesome snacks (they'd left me some Chunky Monkey ice cream in the freezer).

I thought about fixing myself a bowl of ice cream but decided to wait until later. Instead, I picked up a magazine and began to leaf through it, keeping one ear out for sounds from upstairs. There were no thumps or cries, and soon I began to relax. My thoughts drifted away from the quiet, peaceful house and across town to a noisy, crowded gym.

The gym was in Stoneybrook Middle School (or SMS), where I am in the eighth grade. Most of my friends were at a party there that night. A farewell party for Mr. Zizmore, one of the math teachers.

Maybe I should stop for a second and introduce myself. My name, in case you haven't guessed, is Claudia. Claudia Kishi. I'm thirteen, and, as I said, I'm in the eighth grade. I'm Japanese-American, and

I've lived in Stoneybrook, Connecticut, all my life. I have an older sister named Janine, who has an IQ the size of Jupiter (she's a certified genius). My dad's an investment banker, not that I have much of a clue about what that means, and my mom's a librarian. *Her* mother, my grandmother Mimi, used to live with us. I was very, very close to Mimi, and it was hard for me when she died. I still miss her and think of her just about every day.

Mimi understood how important art is to me. Art is a huge part of my life. I love making it, thinking about it, looking at it. I can lose myself in making a collage or staring at a van Gogh. I love to explore different kinds of art: sculpting, drawing, painting, and making jewelry. Last week I even did some finger painting, something I hadn't done in awhile. It was a blast!

Mimi would have had her sleeves rolled up and her hands in the finger paint with me. I can't see my mom or dad doing that. They're proud of my artistic talents, but I think it would mean more to them if I were an exceptional student like Janine.

That will happen when pigs sprout wings.

I don't *hate* school, but I don't see the point of most of the stuff we learn. Take math. I can't understand what all those Xs and Ys have to do with real

life. And I definitely believe that good spelling is overrated as an important skill. I mean, my spelling is about as bad as it gets, but people seem to understand what I'm writing about. Most of the time. My friends do, anyway.

Not that I'm so sure about who my friends *are* these days. My oldest friends, Kristy Thomas and Mary Anne Spier, are still good buds. But my *best* friend, Stacey McGill? Things just aren't the same with her lately.

In fact, things have changed a lot. I guess we're not best friends anymore. We weren't even speaking to each other until recently. We're talking again now but not the way we used to talk. When we were best friends, we could talk about absolutely anything. I trusted her with my deepest, darkest secrets, and she trusted me with hers. Plus, we used to make each other laugh; we could giggle together for hours. These days, we talk more the way Janine and I talk. That is, we're pleasant to each other, but sort of polite.

It feels weird. Very weird.

Stacey and I bonded instantly when she first moved to Stoneybrook from New York City. We share a love of fashion, and we both adore shopping. I thought Stacey was the coolest, most sophisticated girl I'd ever known. Our friendship lasted through all kinds of tough times too — her parents' divorce and Mimi's death and when Stacey had some trouble with her diabetes.

So what happened? I'm almost embarrassed to tell you. But here goes.

A boy came between us. A boy named Jeremy. Jeremy Rudolph. He's new at SMS, and he's the cutest, sweetest guy in school. I had a major, major crush on him from the moment I first saw him. And Stacey knew it. But did that stop her from going out with him?

Take a guess.

According to her, it's not her fault. See, she had a crush on him too. And when he asked her out, after telling her that he saw me as "just a friend," how could she say no?

Excuse me. I'm getting mad just thinking about it. Sometimes I still can't believe that Stacey would stoop so low.

By the way, did I mention that she already *had* a boyfriend when she moved in on Jeremy? She was going out with this guy Ethan, who lives in New York. I guess she didn't have any more loyalty to him than she did to me. She *says* that she and Ethan had decided to cool it for awhile just before Jeremy asked her out. Sure.

Anyway, she and I had this absolutely *humongous* fight. She said some really awful things to me, things I'll never be able to forget. And I guess I slammed into her too. To be honest, I think there were problems in our friendship before Jeremy ever came along. Maybe we would have had that fight eventually even if he hadn't entered the picture.

Ever since then, we've spent a lot of time avoiding each other. But I refuse to avoid Jeremy. He and I are friends, whether Stacey likes it or not. We can really *talk* to each other. I like his company and he likes mine. To tell you the truth, I think he and I have more in common than he and Stacey do — but I'm not going to go there. He's Stacey's boyfriend, and I am trying to accept and respect that.

Especially since Stacey and I sort of made up recently. We're trying to get past the Jeremy incident and be friends again, but I have a feeling it's not going to be easy. As you might be able to tell, I still feel pretty angry at her sometimes. And I think she's still mad at me too. She thinks I should be more understanding. If Jeremy didn't want to go out with me, what did it matter if she went out with him? That's her way of seeing things.

So. All of this may help explain why I didn't mind missing the party that night. How much fun would it have been to watch Stacey and Jeremy having a blast together all evening? Sitting for the Rodowskys sounded like a much better time. For that matter, sitting on a beehive sounded like a better time!

I smiled to myself — just as I heard the front door open. I glanced at my watch. Time had flown. Mr. and Mrs. Rodowsky were already home, and I hadn't even dug into the Chunky Monkey or finished looking at *Vogue*. Instead, I'd been spacing out and thinking about Stacey and Jeremy. Oh, well. I yawned and stretched and stood up to welcome the Rodowskys.

Half an hour later, I was in the kitchen at my house, having a late-night snack and staring at a note my mom had left for me. It said Mary Anne had called about fifteen minutes earlier and that I should call her first thing in the morning. She had "big news."

Darn. Why was Mary Anne's father so strict about late-night phone calls? There was nothing I could do but go to bed, wondering what the "big news" might be. . . .

Chapter 2

I woke up bright and early on Sunday morning. Well, maybe most people wouldn't consider ten-thirty "bright and early," but for me it is. You're *supposed* to sleep in on weekend mornings. It's, like, a law of nature or something. I'll never understand Janine, who thinks it's fun to wake up at the crack of dawn for an early Saturday morning breakfast with her study group. You'll never catch me comparing chemistry lab notes at eight A.M. (You probably wouldn't catch me doing that *any* time, but that's beside the point.)

As soon as I opened my eyes, I remembered Mary Anne's "big news." I decided to head to her house right after breakfast. I thought I could smell pancakes on the griddle downstairs, and my stomach was rumbling.

I pulled on my favorite old cargo pants and a thermal shirt I'd tie-dyed in all the colors of the sunset and went downstairs. Sure enough, my dad was at the stove, flipping pancakes. "Good morning," he said. "Three or four?"

"Five," I answered. "I'm starving." I held out a plate, and he flipped a stack of blueberry pancakes onto it.

"Didn't they feed you over at the Rodowskys' last night?" he asked with a grin. "I thought they always had Ben & Jerry's on hand for you."

I've made a point of telling my parents about the good stuff *other* families have in their freezers and fridges and cupboards. Why? Because my folks don't believe in junk food. My mom's idea of a treat is a perfectly ripe cantaloupe.

I, on the other hand, *do* believe in junk food. Doritos rule, and nothing beats a Mallomar. If anyone ever developed a junk-food scope that could detect sugary, salty, greasy, *yummy* snacks, the meter would go wild in my room. I've hidden that kind of stuff all over. There are Snickers bars in my sock drawer, Gummi Bears behind the books on my bookshelf, and M&M's under the mattress.

"They had ice cream, but I passed on it," I told my dad.

He raised his eyebrows and reached out to feel my forehead. "Are you feeling okay?" he asked.

I laughed. Then I sat down at the table for some serious pigging out.

The pancakes were terrific. I told my dad so as I brought my plate to the sink and rinsed it off. He asked what I was doing that morning. "I'm going over to Mary Anne's," I answered.

"Her new house must be almost finished. You'll miss having her next door," he said.

He was right. It had been fun having Mary Anne so nearby. It was sort of like old times. When she and Kristy and I were little kids, we all lived here on Bradford Court. Then they moved away, Kristy to live across town in this huge mansion that belongs to her new stepfather, and Mary Anne to a big old farmhouse that belonged to her stepmother.

I say "belonged" because that farmhouse doesn't exist anymore. It burned to the ground not long ago, which was traumatic for Mary Anne. Now her family is rebuilding, and while they're waiting to move in to the new house they're living next door to me. (My neighbors are away for a year, so Mary Anne's family is renting their house temporarily.)

As I crossed my yard to Mary Anne's, my curios-

ity began to grow. What was her big news about? I had a funny feeling — but I tried not to think about it.

She answered the door when I knocked. "So?" I asked. "What is it?"

Mary Anne took a breath. "You know how I hate gossip," she began.

It was true. Mary Anne is a very sensitive, caring person. She doesn't like to talk about people behind their backs. "I know," I said. "But you're going to tell me anyway, aren't you?"

She gave me a tiny smile. "Come on in," she said, leading me up to her room.

When we were settled in on a comfy window seat, she said, "It's about Stacey and Jeremy."

"I knew it!" I exclaimed.

Mary Anne looked startled. "You did? Who did you hear it from?"

"Nobody. I mean, I still don't know exactly what you're going to tell me."

"They broke up."

"Wow," I said, trying to take it in. My stomach felt strange and my heart was racing.

Mary Anne nodded. "I know. See? I told you it was big news."

"So tell me more," I said. "Who broke up with who?" Suddenly, this piece of information seemed very, very important.

She shrugged. "I'm not sure, but I think it was mutual. They seemed fine with it. They stayed at the party, but they didn't hang out with each other. And it looked like they were both having a good time."

I could picture Stacey talking with other boys. Had Jeremy talked with other girls?

I swallowed. "Jeremy didn't seem upset?"

Mary Anne shook her head. "Not really. He was just hanging out, joking around with the guys — you know."

So maybe he hadn't talked with other girls.

Would he have talked with me if I'd been there?

Should I even be thinking about it? After all, the breakup wasn't about me. It was between Stacey and Jeremy, and it didn't have anything to do with me.

Did it?

Mary Anne and I talked for awhile more, about the breakup and the dance and how it had felt for her to be there alone (she recently broke up with her longtime boyfriend, Logan Bruno). Finally, she told me she'd promised to help her dad with some errands. "Are you okay?" she asked as I left. "I mean,

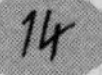

I can understand that you might feel a little strange about all of this."

"Thanks, but I'm fine," I said. "And thanks for letting me know about it." We hugged, and I headed home to think.

In my room, I took out my watercolors and set up a big pad of newsprint on my easel. Sometimes drawing or painting helps me when I need to think. When I make art, I'm relaxed. And when I'm relaxed, I can figure things out.

Sometimes.

Not that morning, though. As I dipped my brush into the paint and created swirls of color, my thoughts continued to race. I didn't know how to deal with what I'd just heard from Mary Anne. Normally, whenever something important happened to me, the first thing I would do was call Stacey. My best friend.

But I couldn't call Stacey. In fact, I didn't even want to. She and I couldn't talk the way we used to — especially about this subject.

I couldn't call Jeremy either.

I would have liked to. If I were really his friend, I would have called. And I am his friend. (I almost reached for the phone.) Unless . . . could I be something more? (I pulled my hand back.)

Jeremy had made it very clear that he didn't like me in that way. He cared about me, I knew that. But he didn't *like* like me. He was only interested in me as a friend.

But . . . that was before we'd gotten to know each other better. My thoughts drifted to some of the phone conversations we'd had recently, in which we'd talked about anything and everything. I remembered the biography project we'd worked on together at school and thought about all the things we'd learned about each other.

I felt my heart racing again. Maybe Jeremy had changed his mind. Maybe he *was* interested in me in that other way. Maybe — maybe that was why he had broken up with Stacey.

The thought made me so agitated that I knocked over my glass of water. As I raced to the bathroom for towels to clean up the mess, I scolded myself. I had to forget about Jeremy and what he might be thinking. I'd know soon enough, when I saw him. In the meantime, there was no point in torturing myself.

But I did. I tortured myself. All day long, I kept thinking about Jeremy. I pictured his soft brown eyes and the way his hair (also a delicious brown) flops across his forehead. I thought about the leather

shoelace with one red bead that he wears on his right wrist. . . .

By dinnertime I was a wreck, and I couldn't hide it. I tried to act normal, but I was too distracted. Finally, after I passed the butter when Janine had asked for the salt, my mom asked me what was wrong.

"Wrong?" I repeated. "Nothing's wrong. I just — I was just thinking about — " Suddenly I remembered something I'd forgotten to tell my parents on Friday. " — the project I volunteered for. It starts tomorrow."

"What is it?" my dad asked.

"It's a new program where kids from SMS are going to work with people who just moved here from other countries," I told him.

"Immigrants?" my dad asked.

"Right," I said. I'd forgotten the exact word. "Immigrants. Anyway, most of them don't speak English very well. They need help, not just learning English but also learning how to live in this country. Like, how to shop for food and stuff. So Erica and I volunteered." Erica Blumberg is a new friend of mine.

I could tell my parents were very impressed. So

was Janine. All three of them offered help if I needed it. As I helped clear the table, I was glad I'd remembered the project. Maybe it would take my mind off —

The phone rang, just as I was putting my plate into the dishwasher. Janine answered it as my heart started knocking around in my chest.

"It's for you." Janine handed me the phone.

"H-hello?" I said, hoping to hear Jeremy's voice.

But it was Erica. And that was the only phone call for me that night. I went to bed knowing I'd have to wait until school the next day to find out where things stood between Jeremy and me.

Chapter 3

I may have gone to bed, but that doesn't mean I went to sleep. Instead, I tossed and turned for hours. I probably dozed off now and then, but mostly I just lay in bed thinking.

Somewhere between eleven and midnight I thought about the way Jeremy walks with a little swing to his step and his habit of flipping back the hair that hangs down over his eyes.

From midnight until two I thought about how lucky I am to have Jeremy as a friend. I know he would stand by me, no matter what. With most people, it can take a long time to create a friendship that strong. But Jeremy and I seem to have a special bond.

I must have slept for awhile between two and three, but then between three and four I thought a lot about the meaning of Jeremy and Stacey's breakup.

Now that they weren't a couple anymore, everything would be different.

But — different how? That was the question.

From four until five I started to think about what it would be like to see Jeremy at school the next day. What would we say? How would we act?

Once I started to think about that, I gave up on any thought of sleeping. Why? Because I had to figure out what to wear. It's not that I'm shallow. I know that it's what's inside that counts, and that appearances mean nothing. I know that a positive attitude and a friendly spirit are much more meaningful than the way a person dresses.

Still.

Clothes are important to me. *Very* important. Think of it this way: We all have to wear clothes every day, right? So we might as well let those clothes make a statement. Clothes are one way we have of telling the world who we are.

I am an artist, a person who values creativity. My clothes reflect that. For me, deciding what to wear can be an art form, just like drawing or painting. And deciding what to wear for a special occasion is like creating a painting for a big museum. The stakes are higher, and you have to make an extra effort to do your best.

Monday was a *very* special occasion. I wanted my outfit to reflect the true and total essence of Claudia. When Jeremy saw me, he would know exactly who I am. It was a lot to ask of a bunch of fabric and thread.

By the time my alarm went off at seven, I had a pretty good idea of what I might wear. I'd come up with an outfit that was attractive yet informal. Relaxed but not grubby. Offbeat but not too weird.

In other words, perfect.

But when I got out of bed to pull together the items I'd need, they didn't look right after all. I tried on outfit after outfit.

"Claudia, breakfast is ready," my mom called from downstairs.

"Coming!" I called back, pulling off a dress. It looked too fussy, too much like I was *trying*. The perfect outfit should look effortless.

"Claudia," my mom called again a few minutes later. "Your eggs are cold. And you should be leaving in five minutes."

Five minutes! I panicked. I opened my closet and pulled out armloads of clothing, sorting through it quickly and tossing things into three piles: "yes," "no," and "maybe."

The "no" pile was the biggest. Next was the

"maybe" pile. And the "yes" pile? Practically nonexistent.

"What, may I ask, are you doing?"

I looked up from my sorting to see Janine leaning on the doorframe.

"Just trying to figure out what to wear," I said, feeling exhausted.

"Special day?"

I nodded, surprised that Janine would understand that a special day demands a special outfit. She's not at all into clothes.

"How about that blouse you made from Mimi's silk kimono?" she asked. "You look beautiful in that."

I stared at her. Then I ran to the closet. The blouse was hanging there, clean and pressed. I pulled it on, then headed back to the "yes" pile for a swirly, short black rayon skirt. Janine, still watching, nodded.

"Excellent," she said.

I checked the mirror. The black chopsticks in my hair complemented the kimono blouse perfectly. I was all set.

Just then, my mom passed my door. "Claudia!" she said. "I thought you'd left already. You'll never be able to walk to school in time now!"

She glanced into my room and saw the mess I'd made. A little smile crossed her face. "You look nice," she said. "How about if I give you a ride?"

Fifteen minutes later, my mom dropped me off in front of the main entrance to SMS. I bolted for my locker, hoping that Jeremy hadn't already passed by. His homeroom is in the same hall as my locker, so I see him nearly every morning.

I put my jacket away, then leaned casually against my locker, waiting. What would I say to him? I practiced a few possibilities in my mind. *So, I heard you broke up. How does it feel to be free at last? Looking for a new girlfriend, by any chance?*

I decided to be quiet and see what Jeremy had to say. I waited, excited and very, very nervous.

Finally, I spotted him walking down the hall in the middle of a crowd of boys. His hair looked shiny and clean, and he was wearing a red corduroy shirt that went beautifully with his eyes.

He saw me at the same time I saw him.

He smiled.

He gave me a wave.

Then he walked on by.

I felt one of the chopsticks fall out of my bun. And I felt my heart drop to the floor.

That wasn't what I'd expected.

All the time I had figured that now Jeremy and I would either be:

A) Friends, or

B) More Than Friends.

I hadn't even considered possibility

C) Less Than Friends.

Chapter 4

Why hadn't Jeremy stopped to talk?

Why, why, why?

I worked this question over all morning. First, during homeroom, I convinced myself that he'd broken up with Stacey because he wanted to go out with someone else — but that someone else was not me. I always like to get the *really* negative thinking out of the way first.

During my first class, math, I managed to start thinking more positively. Maybe he'd been late for class. Or he had been preoccupied with thoughts about some project he was working on. Maybe he didn't want to talk unless we could really *talk*.

All through social studies I made up conversations in my head, conversations that Jeremy and I might have. In my imagination, he and I talked so easily about the situation.

By lunchtime, I had decided that the only reason he hadn't stopped to talk was because it was just too early in the morning. He'd looked sort of sleepy, when I thought about it. Most likely he just hadn't been in the mood to talk.

As I entered the cafeteria, I scanned the tables for Jeremy. When I saw him across the room, I felt a little jolt in my stomach. He was sitting with a bunch of guys, guys I've known for years. Pete Black was there and Alan Gray (the most obnoxious boy in our school — maybe in our universe) and Trevor Sandbourne (an old boyfriend of mine — *very* cute). Cary Retlin, who has lived in Stoneybrook for only awhile, was there too. Cary's very mischievous, and always has a few tricks up his sleeve. I wondered how much those guys knew about what was going on with Jeremy's love life. Do guys talk about stuff like that? It's hard to imagine.

I caught Jeremy's eye and gave him a wave. He smiled at me and waved back.

But did he stand up and start walking toward me?

No.

And did he wave me over to sit at his table?

Nope.

He turned back to Alan and started talking again, ignoring me completely.

Whoa.

I just stood there for a moment, staring. I was having a hard time understanding what had just happened. But it was obvious. Jeremy didn't want to talk to me now any more than he had in the morning.

"What's the matter, Claud?"

Erica was behind me.

"You look like you just saw a ghost," she continued. "What are you looking — oh." She followed my glance and saw Jeremy.

Erica knew how I felt about him. And she knew he and Stacey had broken up. She tugged at my sleeve. "Stop staring, Claudia," she whispered. "Come on."

I shook my head in order to clear it and followed her to the hot-lunch line. I don't even buy hot lunches, but I followed her anyway. I was in a daze.

"Have you talked to him?" she asked as she accepted a plate of macaroni and cheese.

I shook my head.

"So you don't know what's going on yet?" She chose an orange from the fruit display.

I shook my head again.

Erica nodded and picked up a carton of chocolate milk.

"What about Stacey? Have you talked to her?"

One more head-shake.

She raised her eyebrows. "No wonder you're a mess," she said. "Although, I must say you look awesome today." She gave my outfit an appreciative glance. "Come on, let's sit down." She paid for her meal and picked up her tray. Then she turned to scan the cafeteria again. "There's Stacey, sitting with Rachel."

I spotted Stacey. She was talking and laughing with a new friend, Rachel Griffin. She didn't look like someone who had just gone through a devastating breakup.

"I — I don't think I'm ready to talk to her," I said. My feelings were so complicated. I was still hoping to work things out with Stacey and be her friend again, but that was going to take some time.

"Then let's sit with Kristy and Mary Anne and Abby," suggested Erica. She led me through the cafeteria to their table.

"Beautiful outfit, Claudia," Mary Anne said as she moved over to make space for me. "Have you talked to him yet?"

"Talked to who?" Kristy interrupted. "Jeremy?"

"Shhh!" I said.

"What?"

I looked around. "Somebody might hear you."

"So?" said Kristy. "Everybody knows they broke up." Mary Anne gave Kristy a Look. "What? Come on, it's common knowledge. And it's not like Stacey's too upset about it. After all, Ethan was there to comfort her," said Kristy.

I glanced at Mary Anne.

"I forgot to tell you," she said. "Ethan was at the party."

"That must have been interesting for Stacey," Abby put in. "Wasn't that math teacher there too? The one she had the humongous crush on?"

"Mr. Ellenburg?" I asked.

Mary Anne nodded. "It sounds as if he's going to be teaching here again. And guess who else turned up at the party. Toby, that guy she met in Sea City."

"Get out," I said. I glanced at Stacey. She must have had one very wild night. I would have loved to hear about it from her. But we weren't talking that way yet. Maybe someday soon I'd hear the whole story. And maybe I'd find out what was going on between her and Ethan. Were they back together? Was that why she'd broken up with Jeremy?

Jeremy. For a few seconds I'd been able to forget

about him. But just thinking of his name gave me a knot in my stomach. I glanced at his table and saw him laughing and pounding Alan on the shoulder. Alan had probably just done something gross or stupid, like throwing a pat of butter up in the air so it would stick on the ceiling.

Then I glanced at Stacey again. She and Rachel were deep in conversation. She was probably telling Rachel what had happened at the party.

I had thought my troubles would be over if Jeremy and Stacey broke up. Instead, I felt even more mixed up. And I missed talking to both of them.

Just then, the bell rang. As soon as Erica and I left the cafeteria, she turned to me. "I have to tell you something," she said. "I had another fight with my parents last night."

"About the search?" I asked. Erica was adopted, and lately she has begun to wonder about her birth parents, especially her mother. She loves her adoptive family very much, but she is curious about her biological roots. Her parents (the ones who adopted her) understand, but they think she should wait until she's eighteen to search for her birth mother.

Erica nodded. "I know they mean well. But they can't understand what it's like. Only other adopted people can." She looked upset.

I reached out to pat her shoulder. “So what will you do?” I asked.

“I don’t know. Last night I even went on-line and checked out some of the adoption-search sites. They have all these stories and pictures of families who were reunited. Not every story has a happy ending, but I still want to try.”

“Do the sites help you find birth parents?”

She nodded. “They can. But you have to fill in all this information about yourself. I’m not ready to do that behind my parents’ backs. That wouldn’t be right.”

“Wow, that must be so hard,” I said, trying to put myself in Erica’s place. “Is there anything I can do to help?”

“It’s great to be able to talk to you about it,” Erica replied. “That’s enough for now.”

We’d reached the computer lab by then, and I followed Erica in. I was glad at least *one* person wanted to talk to me.

Chapter 5

"Is pretty. So pretty!"

Mrs. Yashimoto was nodding at my kimono blouse. "Thank you," I said. "It was my grandmother's."

She smiled, but I could tell she didn't understand.

"*Arigato,*" I said, remembering one of the few Japanese words I learned from Mimi. *Arigato* means "thank you."

She beamed at me. We'd gotten off to a good start.

It was Monday, after school. And for the first time in what seemed like days, I wasn't thinking about Stacey or Jeremy. Instead, I was concentrating on getting to know the Yashimotos, the family who needed my help learning English and adjusting to life in America.

As soon as the last bell had rung, Erica and I had headed for the home economics room, where we were going to meet our families for the first time. During our training sessions, Ms. Beckwith had gone over the basics of how ESL (that's English as a Second Language) is taught. She'd explained that our job would be to help the families use what they were learning. It would be less threatening, for example, for immigrants to practice English with us than with strangers in a store or a restaurant or a state office. We were helping them polish their skills for the "real world."

The adult volunteers — some of them were teachers from SMS and some were parents or other community members — were responsible for the real teaching, Ms. Beckwith had assured us. Each SMS student was paired with one of the adult volunteers. I'd be working with a woman named Mary Buckley, who had been teaching ESL for years.

That was a relief. I'd been more than a little nervous about what was expected of me. After all, I barely knew any Japanese. Mimi, who spoke it fluently, had taught me to count to ten and say a few other words and phrases, but other than that I knew nothing.

Ms. Beckwith reassured me. "You'll be surprised," she said. "People are people all over the world, and language is not as much of a barrier as you would think."

Ten minutes into my first session with the Yashimotos, I had to admit she was right.

Ms. Buckley — who had told me to call her Mary — had already met several times with the Yashimotos, so she had handled the introductions when they arrived in the classroom.

"This is Mr. Yashimoto," she said, gesturing toward a handsome man in a gray suit. He nodded to me — sort of a little bow — and I nodded back.

"And this is Claudia Kishi," Mary told him, gesturing toward me.

"Please meet you," he said.

Mary smiled at him. "Good," she said. "Almost right. Want to try again?"

He thought for a second. "Please *to* meet you," he said with a question in his voice. He was looking at Mary, not at me.

"Better," she said. "But say 'pleased' instead of 'please.' "

"Ah!" he said. "Okay. *Pleased* to meet you," he told me with confidence.

"And I'm pleased to meet you," I said, remembering to speak clearly but in my normal rhythm. I also made an effort not to shout; during our training we'd been reminded that our students are not hard of hearing. (Many people have a habit of raising their voices when they speak to someone who doesn't speak English.)

Mr. Yashimoto smiled and nodded again.

"And this is Mrs. Yashimoto," Mary said. "She speaks less English, but she's learning quickly."

Mrs. Yashimoto was a small, very pretty woman with shiny dark eyes and a heart-shaped face. She smiled a quick, shy smile that lit up her face. "Hello," she said in a soft voice. Then she gestured toward her two children.

One was a boy of about six. He was *adorable*. His straight black hair was cut short with bangs across his forehead. He gave me a solemn look.

"This — Yoshi-chan," said Mrs. Yashimoto.

I remembered that Mimi used to refer to me as Claudia-chan. "Chan" is sometimes added to a child's name in Japan. "Hello, Yoshi," I said, smiling. "I'm Claudia."

He ducked his head and hid behind his mother.

I smiled at Mrs. Yashimoto. I could see that Yoshi was shy, and I wanted his mom to know I understood that.

She smiled back. Then she nodded toward her little girl, who looked about eight. "Maiko-chan," she said.

Maiko was, if possible, even cuter than Yoshi. Her black hair was fixed in pigtails with pink ribbons, and she wore a pink dress with smocking across the front. She stared at me. "Are you Japanese?" she asked.

I was surprised. She had a strong accent, but her English was excellent. Then I remembered Ms. Beckwith telling us that sometimes younger children pick up languages faster than adults. Also, I remembered that most Japanese children study English in school. Mr. and Mrs. Yashimoto had grown up in a rural area, according to what Mary had said, and had only studied English for a few years, long ago. But their children had been born in Tokyo, and both of them had already been in school for at least a year or two.

"Yes — I mean, I'm Japanese-American," I answered. Maiko certainly wasn't as shy as her brother. "I was born here in the United States. But my grandparents were born in Japan."

Maiko turned to her mother and translated. I recognized the words *oba san* and *oji san* and remembered that they mean "grandmother" and "grandfather." Mrs. Yashimoto nodded and smiled.

"Well," said Mary. "Now that we've all met, I think Mr. Yashimoto and I will begin our lesson over there." She waved toward an unoccupied table in the back of the room. "The children can play with the toys I brought, over there," she said, gesturing toward a nearby corner, "and, Claudia, you and Mrs. Yashimoto can work together right here."

I gulped.

Mary had explained, before the Yashimotos arrived, that Mr. Yashimoto was looking for a job and needed lots of help with skills such as filling out applications and answering interview questions. Mrs. Yashimoto, who was going to stay at home with the children for awhile, needed help with skills such as answering the telephone, shopping for food, and talking to teachers. Mary thought I would be able to help her while she worked with Mr. Yashimoto. We had gone over some of the techniques I'd learned in training, but I was still nervous about being someone's teacher — especially when that someone was older than me.

Mrs. Yashimoto didn't seem to notice my hesitation. She settled the children in with the toys and crayons Mary had brought, then joined me at our table. She looked at me expectantly.

I cleared my throat and paused.

That's when she told me how pretty my blouse was. I knew it took a lot for her to do that. According to Mary, Japanese people don't give gushing compliments the way we do. *"Arigato,"* I said again. Then I looked down at the materials I'd brought with me, things Ms. Beckwith had loaned me for use when I was tutoring. My eye fell on a box of homemade flash cards. I opened it and leafed through them quickly. One of them caught my eye — a card that said *nickel*.

"Money!" I said.

Mrs. Yashimoto gave me a curious look.

I rummaged around in my backpack and pulled out my wallet. "Yes!" I said, opening it to see that there were some bills inside. I took out a ten, a five, and a one. Then I opened the change compartment and shook out some pennies, a nickel, a dime, and a quarter.

"Money," I said again. "Let's learn about money."

Mrs. Yashimoto nodded eagerly and watched to see what I would do next.

I pushed the nickel toward her on the table. "Nickel," I said. "Five cents." I showed her the flash card. And I counted five on my fingers. Then I pointed to her.

"Nickel?" she asked. "Five?"

"Good," I told her. Next, I showed her the dime. "Dime," I said. "Ten cents."

About fifteen minutes later, when we'd finished with the change and moved on to the bills, Maiko interrupted us.

"I'm hungry!" she announced to me. "And Yoshi has to — go."

I nodded. "Okay," I said. "We can take a break. And I think I might have something yummy in my backpack, if it's okay with your mom."

Her eyes lit up. "What do you have?" she asked.

"Let's take Yoshi to the bathroom first," I said. "Can you explain to your mother?" I didn't want Mrs. Yashimoto to wonder where I was going with her little boy.

Maiko translated quickly.

Mrs. Yashimoto looked grateful.

When we returned, I dug out a bag of mini Chips Ahoy cookies from my backpack and showed them to Mrs. Yashimoto. "Okay?" I asked, gesturing toward Maiko and Yoshi. She nodded, smiling. I turned the cookies over to Maiko. "Share them with your brother," I told her.

"I will," she promised. "Will you look at my picture?"

I glanced at Mrs. Yashimoto, who was looking through the flash cards we'd just used, murmuring to herself as she checked each one. "Sure," I said. Maiko grabbed my hand and dragged me to the corner where she'd been playing.

People are people, and kids are kids. It was easy to get along with Maiko, and even Yoshi warmed up to me in a little while. After I'd admired their pictures and given them some ideas about what to draw next, I went back to Mrs. Yashimoto.

"You like children," she said, smiling.

"Yes," I answered, smiling back.

By the end of our lesson, I'd become a lot more confident about being able to teach English. And Mrs. Yashimoto was eager for her next shopping trip. Teaching ESL was going to be a blast.

When I talked to Erica afterward, she agreed. The family she was working with was Bosnian, and she had invited them to her family's house for dinner. I thought that was a great idea and decided to do the same with the Yashimotos. I had a feeling they'd get along beautifully with my parents and Janine.

Chapter 6

Of course, the not-thinking-about-Jeremy thing didn't last. By Tuesday morning, he was on my mind again.

Big time.

Why? Because of the posters plastered all over school. They must have gone up on Monday night or early Tuesday. Either way, they appeared like mushrooms after the rain, all over the place. They came in every shade of pink and red. They were covered with hearts and flowers and lace. And every one of them was a big, shouting reminder to me that I'd better figure out the Jeremy situation — and soon.

The posters were advertising an upcoming dance being thrown by the seventh-graders.

The Cupid's Arrow Dance.

Eek.

Not that I have anything against dances. I don't. Under the right circumstances, I love going to a dance. I've gone to them with friends. I've gone to them alone. And I've gone to them with dates. I like dressing for dances, I like decorating the gym for dances, I like helping to choose the music for dances. And I love to dance!

I might have skipped the dance if Jeremy and Stacey had been going to it together. But now that they had broken up, I had nothing to worry about, right?

Wrong.

I had plenty to worry about. Like: Was Jeremy going to ask me to the dance? If he did, would we be going as friends — or as *more* than friends? If he didn't ask me, should I ask him? What if he — ugh! — asked someone else?

I didn't know what to do. It seemed as if those posters were *everywhere*. I couldn't forget about the dance for a second. And as the week went by, more posters appeared. There was one by my locker and one in the hall near my homeroom. They were plastered all over the cafeteria. By Thursday, there was even one in the girls' room!

Meanwhile, Jeremy seemed to be avoiding me. I used to see him every morning. He'd stop to chat as he passed my locker. But now he must have been taking a different route to his homeroom — or maybe it was just that I wasn't hanging out at my locker as much. I guess I was avoiding him a little too. I didn't know how to act around him.

Jeremy is in my English class, which used to make me happy. Now it just made me nervous. I would bury my nose in a book until I was sure he had come in and taken his seat. And I would bolt out of the room the second the bell rang.

School was becoming a very stressful place.

I would have loved to talk to Stacey (who, I'd heard, was thinking about asking Ethan to the dance), but how could I? For one thing, we were hardly on close speaking terms yet. And for another, I *definitely* wasn't ready to talk to her about my feelings for Jeremy.

Erica would have been glad to listen, but I didn't want to strain our new friendship by babbling on too much about my problems. I knew she had plenty on her mind anyway. She'd told me she thought I should just invite Jeremy. I hemmed and hawed.

Finally, by Thursday, I was driving *myself* crazy

with all my indecision. I realized it was time to take action.

I decided to ask Jeremy to the dance after all.

Just *ask* him. What was the worst that could happen? He could say no. And I would deal with that.

Eek.

But how and when should I ask him? Should I just approach him casually? I'd have to catch him when he was alone, which wasn't easy during school. No way did I want Alan Gray to overhear and start teasing me.

Maybe I could call him at home. That could work. Unless his mother answered the phone. If he wasn't there, she'd expect me to leave a message. What would I say? "Uh — tell him Claudia wants to know if he wants to go to the dance with . . ."

Um, no thanks.

Finally, I came up with the perfect solution.

I would write him a note.

I raced home after school on Thursday, eager to put my thoughts down on paper. I'd discovered the perfect way to find out what was going to happen between Jeremy and me.

After a quick snack of Combos and a mini Snickers bar, I sat down at my desk and pulled out a sheet of my best stationery. Across the top is a painting by Monet, of beautiful water lilies floating on a pond.

Dear Jermy,

I wrote. Something looked not quite right about Jeremy's name, but I didn't stop to think about it. The important thing was to write from my heart.

I am writting this note to ask you an imporetant questium. You can say no if you want

I stopped and thought for a second. Then I crumpled up the paper and threw it in my wastebasket. Why should I tell him he could say no? First of all, he knew that. Second of all, why put ideas in his head? I should think positive. I started over.

Dear Jermery,
I have ben thinking a lot about you. and wundering if you would like to go to the dance with me. As a date. Or not. Maybe just as freinds. Or maybe as

Ugh! This was harder than I'd thought it would be. I crumpled up that try too. Then I started again, but this time I was smart about it. I used a piece of paper from my science notebook instead of wasting my good stationery. I could always copy it over onto the Monet paper later, once I'd figured out what to say.

Dear Jerymy,
I know we havent' talked in awile, but I still think of you as a good freind. Would you like to go to the danse with me? As a freind, that is. Or as my date. Or both. Or

Another piece of paper bit the dust. My wastebasket was filling up quickly. I sat and thought for a couple of minutes, tapping my pencil against my teeth. Then I pulled out another sheet of paper and started again. Maybe I should try to be funny.

Dear Jermie,
Remember me, your good freind Claudia? Ha-ha. Just kidding. Anyway,

Or maybe not. Being funny wasn't so easy for me, especially about something that was so important. Maybe Abby could write a funny note to a boy she had a crush on, but not me. It was probably better just to come out and say what I was thinking.

Dere Jaramy,

I have been trying to figure out how to ask you to the Cuspid's Arow Dance. This seams like the easyest way. Would you like to go with me? We could go as freinds, or maybe as more-than-freinds. Eether way would be fine with me, as long as we can hang out and talk a little. I have always licked talking with you. You seem to understand me in a specail way, and I think I udnerstand you too . . .

I stopped writing and stared at the words I'd put down so far. They seemed a little bold — but I also liked how straightforward the note sounded. If Jeremy read this, he would know exactly how I was feeling. (Well, not *exactly*. I would much rather go to the dance as more-than-friends, but I didn't have to spell that out.)

I liked how this note was turning out. But I had a nagging feeling that some of the words weren't spelled quite right. And was the grammar correct? Was I really saying what I meant to say?

That's when I had my brainstorm.

I could type my note into the computer and have the computer spellcheck and grammarcheck the whole thing. Then I could copy it back onto paper, using my good stationery. The note would look perfect, and I wouldn't have to be embarrassed by any mistakes.

I finished writing down my thoughts. Then I turned on my computer and typed the whole thing out (that took me awhile). Finally, I activated my spellchecker.

Yikes!

I know I don't spell well, but sometimes it's still a surprise to see just how badly I mangle some words. It took the computer a long, long time to fix up what I'd written. There were some words it couldn't even figure out, like Jeremy's name! I realized I might not be spelling it right and decided to start the note with "To a good friend," instead.

Grammarcheck didn't take as long, but I was glad I'd thought of doing it. There were some run-on sentences, and the computer had no idea what I meant by "more-than-friends."

But I left that in. I had a feeling Jeremy would know.

Once the computer was sure that everything in the note was perfect, I printed out a copy. Then I pulled out the last sheet of my Monet stationery and carefully, letter by letter, copied the whole thing out in my own handwriting.

I signed my name at the bottom and folded the note into thirds. Then I taped it shut and put it into my backpack, ready for an early morning delivery. I figured I could slip the note into Jeremy's locker first thing, so he'd have it before homeroom. And by the end of the day on Friday, I'd have my answer. I had made my feelings clear, and soon I would know how Jeremy truly felt.

❀ Chapter 7

Another big day. Another clothing crisis.

I woke up on Friday with a weird feeling in my stomach, the feeling you have when you know something big is about to happen. For a second I couldn't remember what it was. Then it came to me.

The Note.

As soon as I remembered, I realized that, once again, I had to figure out the perfect outfit for the occasion.

What do you wear when you're sending a note to a guy you really like, asking him to a dance? I wanted to look just right when Jeremy gave me his answer. I wanted to look like someone he'd want to say yes to.

I started my routine again, pulling out all my clothes and trying on different combinations.

I experimented with an artistic, New York-y, all-black look.

Too dark.

Then I went in another direction and tried on a frilly pink dress one of my aunts had given me.

Too frou-frou.

The dress paired with black leggings and combat boots?

Uh, no.

The combat boots and leggings with a green miniskirt and purple sweater?

Better.

I traded in the boots for a pair of platform sneakers, switched my sweater color to yellow, and added some star-shaped earrings I'd made out of Sculpey.

"Ta-daaa!" I said finally, checking myself one last time in the mirror. I felt good about my outfit.

My mom liked it too. What she didn't like was that I was going to be late unless she drove me to school again. But she was nice about it and even waited while I gulped down a yogurt and double-checked my backpack to make sure I'd remembered The Note.

"It won't happen again!" I promised as I said good-bye to her at SMS.

Tons of kids were still milling around outside,

waiting for the first bell. Thanks to the ride Mom had given me, I had plenty of time to go to Jeremy's locker.

I walked quickly through the halls. Jeremy's locker is near my science classroom. My heart was beating fast as I approached the spot. Was I really going to do this? What if he thought I was crazy? What if he wanted nothing to do with me? What if he'd already asked someone else to the dance?

I stopped near the girls' room and took a few deep breaths. *Relax*, I told myself. *It's not such a big deal. He's only a boy. It's only a dance.*

The deep breathing worked. I managed to calm myself down enough to continue toward Jeremy's locker. As I walked, I kept glancing around nervously, looking over my shoulder to make sure nobody caught me. Then I realized that was silly. After all, I had a right to walk down any hall in SMS.

Still. I didn't want Jeremy to pop up unexpectedly before I'd had a chance to stick The Note into his locker.

Finally, I arrived at the right spot. I wasn't sure of his locker number, but I thought it was three down from the door to my science classroom.

I took one more glance around. A few people

were in the hall: kids, teachers, one of the janitors. But nobody was paying any attention to me.

I slung my backpack around, unzipped it, and pulled out The Note. Then I tried to stick it through one of the vents at the top of the locker.

It wouldn't go in.

Panic!

Glancing around some more, I took the note, folded it in half, and tried again.

It was still too big.

I folded it some more and then it was too thick to fit through the vent. More kids were walking through the halls now. The first bell was going to ring in a few minutes. My heart was thudding away again.

Finally, I managed to shove the thing through the vent. Then I grabbed my backpack and fled to a spot just down the hall, near the water fountain.

I wanted to see Jeremy find The Note.

I wanted to see what happened when he unfolded it and started to read. Would he smile? Would he frown?

Now the hall was full of kids. I wasn't going to have time to go to my own locker before homeroom, but that was okay.

Where was Jeremy?

Suddenly, I had an awful thought. What if he were home sick? I didn't think I could stand to wait through the whole weekend. The suspense would just about do me in.

"Hey, Claud, what are you doing here?"

I whirled around. "Kristy!" I said. "You almost gave me a heart attack."

"A little jumpy this morning?" she asked. "What's up?"

"I — " I started to answer, but just then, out of the corner of my eye, I saw Jeremy appear at the very end of the hall. At the same moment, Erica approached Kristy and me.

"What's going on?" she asked.

"Shhh! Shhh!" I said. "Wait! I mean — " Jeremy was coming closer. Quickly, in whispers, I told them what I had done.

"A note? Cool," said Erica.

"You're asking him to the dance?" said Kristy. "Excellent."

"Shhh! Shhh!" I said again. "You guys, he's going to *hear* you." Suddenly, I could hardly breathe. "I can't look," I said, turning my back and hiding my face in my hands. "Tell me what he's doing."

Kristy put on a sports announcer's voice. "Rudolph is moving quickly down the hall," she reported in a low voice. "He ducks, he weaves, he avoids every person walking the other way. He is amazing!"

"Kristy!" I hissed.

She grinned and kept going. "Now Rudolph is approaching his locker. He comes in for a three-point landing — yes! He's there."

"He's there?" I gulped.

"He's there," whispered Erica.

"Oh my lord," I said. My face felt hot. My back was still turned to him. I just couldn't stand to watch.

"Rudolph dials his combination," Kristy went on. "He dials to the left. To the right. To the left again — and — *yes*! The locker is open."

"Now what's he doing?" I asked. "Did he see the note?"

Erica shook her head. "I don't think so. Not yet."

"Rudolph rummages around, pulling out books and — ew! — an old sneaker. Folks, that sneaker must be from the Paleolithic era. I can just about smell it from here."

"Kristy," I hissed again. "That's enough. Quit it!"

"Quit what?" she asked. "You wanted to know what he was doing."

Just then, Erica gave a little gasp. "He's closing the locker," she said.

"What? What about the note?" I whirled around to look at him. I could hardly believe he'd missed it. But, sure enough, Jeremy was standing there, twirling the lock before he walked off.

Something was wrong. I did a quick count.

His locker was the fifth one down from my science classroom.

Not the third.

"Oh, no!" I groaned.

"What?" asked Kristy. "Claudia, you're all white. Are you okay? Should I call nine-one-one?" Kristy was cracking up. She thought this was a riot.

"What it is, Claud?" Erica asked.

"I was wrong," I said.

"Oh, I don't think so. He'll probably see the note the next time he goes to his locker."

I shook my head. "No, he won't."

"Why?" asked Kristy. She'd stopped laughing.

"Because I put it in the wrong locker."

"You — what?" said Erica.

"I put it in the wrong locker."

"I don't believe this," said Kristy.

"We have to get it back," I said. Suddenly, I remembered everything I'd written in that note. My body went hot, then cold, then hot again. Nobody but Jeremy should see that note.

"Don't worry," said Erica. "We'll help you."

"Sure, we will," said Kristy. "But it'll have to be later. The first bell is going to ring any second."

"No! No! You have to help me now!" I was desperate.

"Okay, calm down," said Kristy. "Let's go check it out. Which locker did you put it in?"

I led them to the locker. "This one," I said. "Maybe a corner of the note is still sticking out." I stood on tiptoe to see. Nothing.

Kristy looked both ways down the hall, which was emptying out as kids headed to homeroom. Then she started twirling the dial and jamming the handle. "Come on, come on!" she said to the locker. "Open up, you dumb thing!"

Guess who ran by us just then.

Stacey.

"What are you guys *doing*?" she asked, coming to a stop.

How on earth was I going to explain this? Luckily, I didn't have to. Kristy took care of that. How? She lied. She told Stacey we were helping with a story for the school paper. The topic was How Secure Are Our Lockers?

"I might know a trick," said Stacey. She reached into her handbag and pulled out a nail file. Then she started to poke at the handle of the locker. After a few attempts, she gave up. "Never mind," she said. "I saw it in a movie once, but they must have faked it."

I slumped over, feeling as if I might start crying.

"I know!" said Kristy. "I know somebody who can definitely open this."

"If you're thinking about the janitor, forget it," said Erica. "He won't open somebody else's locker for you."

"Not the janitor," Kristy said. "Cary Retlin."

Just then, the first bell rang.

It was time for homeroom.

I didn't want to leave the locker, but I had no choice.

I walked away, leaving the note inside.

Chapter 8

Homeroom normally lasts ten minutes. You go in, you sit down, the teacher takes attendance, you hear some announcements over the loudspeaker, and that's it.

That morning, homeroom lasted about thirty million centuries.

I was dying inside. Every time I thought about that note and what it said, every time I thought about someone other than Jeremy reading it, my toes curled up and my stomach started to churn. Thinking about it made me blush too, so I probably looked like a traffic light. First I'd turn red with embarrassment, then green with nausea.

I had to get that note back.

I wasn't sure what I'd do with it if I did get it back. Would I try again to give it to Jeremy? Maybe it would be safer just to destroy it and forget all about inviting him to the dance.

When the bell finally rang, I grabbed my stuff and broke the world's record for the hallway dash. I skidded to a stop in front of That Locker just as Kristy arrived with Cary Retlin in tow.

"Having a little problem?" said Cary, raising one eyebrow in his usual way.

He was getting a big kick out of the situation. "Just open the locker," I said.

He raised the eyebrow even higher.

"Please?" I added.

He smirked a little.

"Hurry!" I said. The hall was already filling up with people. The owner of the locker could arrive any minute.

"As you wish," he said, still wearing the smirk. Then he pushed up his shirtsleeves, turned toward the locker, and fiddled around for about three seconds. He stepped back, and the locker swung open.

I stared at him. "How did you do that?" I asked.

He shrugged. "I could tell you, but then I'd have to erase your memory."

"Claudia," Kristy said in a strange voice. "Never mind how he did it. Guess whose locker this is?"

"What?" I asked. "Whose is it?"

She gestured at the open locker, and I peered inside.

The tiny space was a mess. I saw gym clothes and open notebooks and moldy sandwiches in it. "Looks like a guy's," I observed.

"Not just any guy's," said Kristy. "Check it out." She reached in and gingerly drew out a bizarre-looking pancake-shaped piece of rubber. "Fake vomit," she said.

"Oh, ew!"

She tossed it back in. "I also see a Super Soaker tucked away in the back," she said. "And look at those stickers."

I noticed a bunch of bumper stickers on the inside of the locker. "Warning: I Brake for Donuts," said one. "Gives Peas a Chance," said another. My stomach started churning again. "You don't think — " I began.

Kristy nodded grimly. "I'm afraid so. This locker belongs to — "

"Alan Gray," I chimed in.

We shuddered.

"What's the problem?" asked Cary, who'd been watching us, an amused look on his face. "Alan's a nice guy."

We turned to stare at him.

"Nice?" repeated Kristy. "Sure, he's nice. If you like dorks."

"If your idea of a good time involves a whoopee cushion," I added.

"But I don't want him to see the — " I stopped. How much had Kristy told Cary? If he didn't know about the note, I wasn't about to tell him.

Cary shrugged. "Whatever," he said. "I've done my part. I'm out of here."

"You won't tell Alan we were in his locker, will you?" I asked.

"Probably not," said Cary, shooting me that smirk.

"Cary!" I wailed.

"Okay, I won't. But you owe me." He turned and sauntered down the hall.

"Great," I said, rolling my eyes. "He's the last guy I want to owe anything to."

"That's the least of your problems," Kristy said. She was still staring into the locker.

I didn't like the sound of that. "What do you mean?"

"The note," she said. "I don't see it."

"You don't? But it has to be here. It has to! I just put it here." I felt a wave of panic rise up inside me.

I took a deep breath. "Maybe this isn't the right locker," I said desperately. I looked down the row, counting. "One, two, three — augggh!" There was no question about it. This was the locker I'd put the note into.

Kristy was still rummaging around. "Nope," she reported. "It's just not here."

My stomach stopped churning. Instead, it dropped to the floor. I was in deep, deep trouble.

Alan Gray had The Note.

Kristy stopped poking around in the locker and stood up to face me. We stared at each other in horror.

Just then, one of the loudspeakers crackled with static. Someone was about to make an announcement. I saw Kristy's face turn white, and I know mine was probably even paler than hers. "He wouldn't — " I began.

"He might," Kristy said grimly.

I stood there, paralyzed. Was Alan Gray about to read my note to the whole school?

"Attention, SMS students. Here's an announcement that we missed during homeroom," said a male voice.

I held my breath.

"There will be a daffodil sale in the cafeteria, between eleven and one. Be sure to buy a bunch for your special someone," the voice continued.

I let my breath out and exchanged a relieved look with Kristy.

"And one more thing — " said the voice.

I gulped.

"Think spring!" With that, the loudspeaker clicked off.

I sank down so that I was sitting in the hallway, leaning against the lockers. "I can't take this," I told Kristy, who had joined me on the floor. "What do you think he'll do with the note?"

"He's capable of anything," said Kristy darkly. "He might copy it a hundred times and spread it all over the school. Or he might post it on his Web site. Or — "

"Stop!" I cried. "Forget I asked."

"It'll all work out," said Kristy, trying to comfort me. She patted me on the shoulder. "Don't worry."

Ha. Easy for her to say.

I worried through my morning classes. And I worried between classes as I walked through the halls. I hadn't seen Alan yet that morning. How would he act when we first ran into each other?

Would he laugh out loud? Gloat? Tease me in front of everyone? In a way, I wanted to see him, just to get the worst of it over with.

I finally spotted him coming toward me as I was on my way to the last class of the day. For a second, I considered ducking into the rest room, but the nearest one happened to be a boys' room. I had to face Alan. I had no choice.

I walked toward him, my face on fire. I have never felt so embarrassed in my life.

Alan had a funny look on his face — not the look I was expecting. Instead of a grin, he wore a sheepish half smile. "Hey, Claudia," he said as we drew closer. "Um — can I talk to you?"

This was it.

"Sure," I said. I faced him squarely. "Go on."

"Not here," he said, looking around at all the other kids filling the hall. "How about in there?" He gestured toward a nearby classroom. "I think that room is empty."

"Okay," I said. I stared at the back of his head as he led me into the room. What kind of thoughts were percolating in there? For all I knew, he'd already passed the note along to Jeremy, adding a few sarcastic comments of his own.

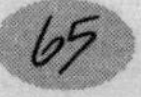

Alan closed the door behind us once we were inside the classroom. Then he turned to me. "Claudia," he began.

I closed my eyes and took a deep breath. *Here it comes,* I thought, tensing all my muscles. I opened my eyes again and met Alan's. His eyes looked strange. Soft. He wasn't grinning.

"Claudia," he said again, hesitantly. "That note." He stopped. He ran a hand through his hair. "That note — it was the nicest thing anyone has ever written to me."

I stared at him.

Oh. My. Lord.

He thought the note was for him. I was totally and completely shocked. "It — " I began. "That note — " I couldn't even form the words. I had to tell him the note wasn't meant for him, but I couldn't seem to speak.

"I know I'm a pain sometimes, Claudia," Alan said earnestly. "And I know your friends think I'm nothing but a clown. But you saw the real me."

"Alan, I — "

He held up a hand. "Let me finish," he said. "You know, I've always admired you, Claudia. You are so creative, so talented. You're . . . you're one in a million." He blushed and looked down at his feet.

"I never thought someone like you would be interested in someone like me. You know, I'm really trying to change, to be better . . . um, more mature."

I studied the top of his head. Suddenly, I realized that Alan Gray was just another boy. It took a lot of guts for him to say this stuff to me. I knew what it took because of how I'd had to psych myself up to write that note.

Alan looked up again and caught me staring. I felt a strange jolt when our eyes met. "So, anyway," he continued. "My answer is yes."

"Yes?" I repeated.

"Yes. I would love to go to the Cupid's Arrow Dance with you."

Chapter 9

A few hours later everybody was gathered in my room for our BSC meeting. Kristy had called the meeting to order at precisely five-thirty. Then, after conducting club business, she'd turned to me. "So, what happened?" she asked. "I'm dying to know. Did you run into Alan? Did he read the note? What did he say?"

I hesitated. I wasn't sure if I was ready to tell everyone the story yet. Fortunately, Mary Anne jumped in. "I heard all about it at lunch, Claudia," she said sympathetically. "I can't believe your note fell into Alan's hands! But don't worry. I bet it will all work out okay."

Kristy snorted. "Sure," she said. "If your idea of 'okay' includes being humiliated in front of the whole school."

"Kristy!" Mary Anne said.

"Sorry," said Kristy, shooting me a little grin. "I'm just kidding. But you never know what Alan will do."

That was for sure. I looked around at my friends, wondering what everyone would think when I told them that Alan and I were going to the Cupid's Arrow Dance together.

Mary Anne would be accepting. She always is.

Stacey might be understanding. She knows how complicated "boy stuff" can be.

Kristy, I knew, would go ballistic. To her, Alan Gray is nothing but a pest. I'm not sure she even considers him human. She's known him, as I have, since kindergarten. And not once have I ever heard her say anything nice about him.

"You're right, Kristy," Stacey said now. "Alan is capable of anything. Remember when he picked up that zit cream that dropped out of Shawna Riverson's pack?"

Kristy nodded, groaning. "He auctioned it off in the cafeteria at lunchtime."

"That was in sixth grade," I protested. "I think Alan's changed a little since then."

Kristy looked at me. "Alan Gray? The guy who wore his underwear on his head for the talent show in fourth grade? The guy who sticks straws up his nose? The guy who once licked the gym floor on a bet — "

"Stop!" I said, holding up a hand. "I know he used to do all that stuff. I'm saying that I think he's matured a little bit recently."

Kristy peered at me suspiciously. "Claudia, why are you defending Alan?"

"Raisinets, anyone?" I asked brightly, holding up a box of candy.

"Yum! I'll take some," said Mary Anne.

I handed them over. "And I have some popcorn for you, Stacey," I added, reaching under my bed to find my secret stash.

"Claudia?" Kristy asked.

"What?" I replied innocently.

"I asked why you're defending Alan Gray." She was staring at me intently as she tapped a pencil on my desk.

"I — " Just then, the phone rang. "I'll get it!" I cried with relief. I reached for the phone. "Hello, Baby-sitters Club."

"Acme Diaper Service here," said a male voice.

It was Alan.

And he was up to his old tricks.

I didn't say a word.

"Claudia?" he asked after a second.

"I'm hanging up," I said.

"No, wait!" he cried. "Wait. I'm sorry. It's just a bad habit. I didn't mean it."

"Okay," I said warily. "What's up?"

"I wanted to thank you again for that note," he said, sounding sincere. "And I wanted to know what color dress you'll be wearing to the dance, so I can buy you a corsage."

I couldn't help feeling touched.

"Who is it?" asked Kristy impatiently. "Is it a wrong number?"

I waved my hand at her. "You're welcome," I said into the phone. "And as for color, I don't know. Red, maybe. I'll let you know."

"Cool," said Alan.

"I have to go now," I told him.

" 'Bye, Claudia," Alan said softly.

I hung up.

"Red *what*?" Kristy asked. "Claudia, who was that?"

"Nobody," I mumbled.

"Claudia," Kristy said warningly.

"ItwasAlan," I said quickly.

Kristy looked puzzled.

"Alan," I said, giving up. "It was Alan Gray, okay?"

Kristy held up her hands. "Fine, fine," she said. "You don't have to get all huffy." She shook her head. "Doesn't he ever get tired of making prank phone calls while we're having meetings?"

"It wasn't exactly a prank," I said. I took a deep breath. It was time to spill the beans. "Actually, he wanted to know what color dress I was planning to wear to the dance."

"Why would he want to know that?" asked Mary Anne, bewildered.

"Because he wants to buy me a corsage," I said bravely. "He's going to be my date. I'm going to the Cupid's Arrow Dance with Alan Gray."

For a few moments, the room was silent.

Then Kristy exploded. "You *what*?" she exclaimed. "Are you out of your mind?" She stared at me for a second. Then she laughed. "Oh, I get it," she said. "This is a joke, isn't it?"

I shook my head. "Nope," I said. "We're just going to the dance together, that's all."

"So you're going to sit here and tell me that Alan Gray is your new boyfriend," Kristy said, folding her arms across her chest.

"Not my boyfriend," I answered. "I never said

that. I just said we're going to the dance together. As a matter of fact, we're going as friends."

"Friends don't buy each other corsages," Kristy pointed out. "And anyway, you and Alan Gray aren't exactly friends."

"Well, maybe we will be after this." I folded my arms too.

Mary Anne and Stacey had been sitting there silently. Finally, Mary Anne spoke up.

"I think it's nice," she said. "Sometimes people aren't what they seem. We have to be open-minded about Alan."

I shot her an appreciative glance. Yea, Mary Anne! She understood.

"I just don't believe this," Kristy said, waving her arms around. "This is Alan Gray we're talking about. *Alan Gray!*"

Stacey giggled. "He is kind of cute, if you think about it."

You know how in cartoons smoke sometimes comes out of people's ears when they're really mad? I thought that was going to happen with Kristy. She glared at Stacey.

"Cute?" she asked. "*Cute?*" She shook her head. "That's it. I give up on you guys." She put her head down on my desk.

We all cracked up.

"So, how did it happen?" Mary Anne asked, leaning forward.

"Did he, like, confess to a secret crush on you?" asked Stacey.

"Not exactly." I explained how he'd thought the note was for him. (I didn't say who the note was originally for — but Stacey could probably guess.) "He was so pleased that I was being nice to him that I couldn't exactly tell him it was for somebody else," I said. Then I told them what he'd said about wanting to be a better person.

Kristy, whose head was still buried in her arms, groaned when she heard that. "And you believe him?" she asked.

"Don't listen to her," Mary Anne told me. "I think that's very sweet." Her eyes looked moist.

"That's what Erica thought," I said. "I told her about it when we walked home from school."

Kristy groaned again. "I can't believe you guys are acting like he's just a normal guy," she said. "Don't you see? This is probably a setup for some huge prank."

For a second, I wondered if she could be right. Then I remembered that soft look in Alan's eyes.

"You're wrong, Kristy," I said. "But it doesn't matter what you think. I'm the one who's going to the dance with him."

"I give up," said Kristy. She glanced at the clock. "Anyway, it's six. This meeting is adjourned."

Soon afterward, Kristy and Mary Anne left. Stacey stayed behind, rearranging some things in her backpack.

"So, Claudia," she said, not looking at me. "What about Jeremy?"

Just hearing his name made my stomach flip over. Jeremy. What about him? I didn't know what to think anymore. In a way, it was easier just to concentrate on Alan. Things with Jeremy were too confusing, too weird. Why had he been avoiding me? Why had I been avoiding him? Were we ever going to end up together? What if he asked me to the dance now?

I would have loved to talk everything over with Stacey — the *old* Stacey. But even though we were speaking to each other again, things weren't the same. I wasn't ready to open up to her. Especially on the topic of Jeremy.

"I don't know, Stace," I said slowly. How could I put it? "I guess I really don't want to talk about Jeremy with you."

I was trying to be nice but firm. I didn't want to have another fight with Stacey, but I wasn't ready to be best buds with her again either.

Stacey stopped fooling with her backpack and glanced up at me. For a second, she looked hurt. Then she nodded. "Fair enough," she said.

She picked up her stuff and walked out the door.

Chapter 10

"*Fair enough.*" But was it really fair that I didn't want to talk to Stacey? And even if it were, did that mean it was right?

Stacey's words echoed in my head as I gazed out the car window. My dad was at the wheel. It was Saturday, and we were headed for New York for a day at the Metropolitan Museum — with the Yashimotos. When they had come over for dinner two nights before, we had begun talking about art (guess who started *that* conversation) and heard that they hadn't yet been to the Met, so my parents and I insisted on taking them there.

As we whizzed down the highway, I couldn't help thinking about Stacey. Usually, when I'm headed to New York, I'm on my way to hang out with her there. We'd done all kinds of fun things when she was in the city visiting her dad: We'd gone to Broadway shows and to the Hard Rock Cafe; we'd explored Greenwich Village and checked out Central Park. Stacey taught me a lot about enjoying New York. In fact, she took me to the Met for *my* first time.

Maybe, I thought, I *wasn't* being fair. Maybe I should have said more to Stacey. Maybe these bad feelings between us weren't going to end until we both opened up a little more. And maybe I could be the one to open up first.

It was something to think about.

Meanwhile, I had to put thoughts of Stacey aside and focus on the Yashimotos. This was a special day for them. They were going to see so many wonderful things.

"Do you like paintings?" I asked Mrs. Yashimoto, who was sitting next to me. We had borrowed Kristy's family's minivan for the day so we could fit everyone into one car. (Everyone, that is, except Janine. She had a study date that afternoon.)

Mrs. Yashimoto looked at me quizzically.

I pulled out a pamphlet I'd brought along, a guidebook to the Met. I pointed to a picture of one of my favorite paintings in the museum, a Degas, showing ballet dancers warming up. "Painting," I said.

"Oh, yes," gasped Mrs. Yashimoto. "I like very much."

"I like it too!" piped up Maiko. "Pretty dancers."

"Is that all they have there?" asked Yoshi. (He had stopped acting so shy around me by then.) His arms were folded across his chest. I could see he wasn't impressed by the Degas.

"No!" I said. "They have *everything*. Paintings and sculptures and pottery and jewelry and whole rooms that show how people used to live. And armor they used to wear too. You'll like that. They even have an entire building inside the museum."

"Building?" asked Mr. Yashimoto from the front seat. He turned to look at me. "What sort of building?"

His English was improving every day. He had been on several job interviews in the past week — and one of them was at my dad's office! It sounded as if he had a good chance of finding a position there.

"A temple," I told him. "The Temple of Dendur. It was a gift of the Egyptian government, and it's in this huge glass room. There's a pool of water near it, in the same spot where the river Nile flowed when the temple was in Egypt."

I knew a lot about the temple because it had become a favorite place for me. Whenever I go to the Met, I spend time there. It's very peaceful, and sometimes you just need a rest after you've been roaming the galleries looking at all the beautiful things.

"Can you swim in the pool?" asked Maiko.

I shook my head, laughing a little. "I don't think so," I said. "It's not that kind of pool. It's not very deep."

Mrs. Yashimoto was smiling, but I could tell she had lost track of the conversation. I had noticed at the dinner at our house that even though she tried hard to listen, sometimes we just went too fast for her. I looked over the pamphlet until I found a picture of the temple with its pool. I showed it to her. "No swimming," I said, pointing to the pool and smiling.

"Ah," she said, nodding. "Maiko love swim."

"Maiko loves swimming?" I asked.

She nodded again. "Maiko loves swimming," she said, carefully echoing the way I'd said it.

"So do I," I told Maiko. "But we're not going to swim today."

"What do you like to do?" my mom asked Yoshi.

"Run!" Yoshi answered loudly. "And play with my ball. And eat ice cream and candy and pizza!"

"He sounds like an American boy already," my mom told Mrs. Yashimoto.

"You like lasagna too, don't you?" I asked. I had helped my mom make lasagna for our dinner. She had been worried about what to make, but I had assured her that the Yashimotos liked to eat "American food," even though lasagna is more Italian than American. Sure enough, Yoshi had asked for seconds.

Our dinner had been interesting. When they arrived, Mr. and Mrs. Yashimoto presented us with a gift — a box of dried fruit that had been wrapped so beautifully that none of us wanted to open it. I knew, from what I had learned about Japanese customs, that this was not out of the ordinary. People always bring presents when they visit, and sometimes they are very extravagant.

They also asked if they should take off their shoes. That may sound weird, but again, it's the custom in Japan. Families take off their shoes when they enter their homes or when they're visiting. (I guess they have to be careful to make sure their socks don't have holes in them.) In schools, kids have outdoor shoes and indoor shoes.

Speaking of school, here's another interesting

Japanese custom. Guess who cleans Japanese schools. The students! For a period of time every day the kids take out brooms and mops and go to work making their school shine. (Kids also take turns serving one another lunch.) Somehow I can't quite imagine American students doing that. But in Japan they're used to it.

The Yashimotos were very polite throughout dinner. They ate everything we offered them, even though I knew some of the food must have seemed strange to them. Did you know that many Japanese people eat fish for breakfast? Sounds yucky, but then they probably think blueberry pancakes are weird.

"Here we are!" said my dad finally, pulling into a parking garage near the museum.

I felt a little tingle of excitement. I have been to the Met many times, but I still haven't seen everything there. The place is *huge*! You could spend a lifetime wandering around, drinking in all the beautiful art.

"I want to see the armor!" cried Yoshi.

"That sounds very interesting," Mr. Yashimoto agreed.

"But what about the pool?" asked Maiko.

"And paintings?" put in Mrs. Yashimoto shyly.

"Maybe we should split up for awhile," my mom suggested. "There are so many of us and there's so much to see. We can meet in an hour or so, just to check in."

That's how I ended up in a roomful of Rodins with Mrs. Yashimoto and Maiko.

That gallery is awesome. It's a long room filled with sculptures by one of the great masters of all time. Rodin — his first name was Auguste — understood the human form very well. He could convey all kinds of emotions through his work.

"Beautiful." Mrs. Yashimoto sighed as she took everything in. She moved among the sculptures, examining each one carefully.

I was gazing at the way Rodin had sculpted a man's arm, trying to understand how he could create muscles that were so real-looking, when I heard an argument behind me.

"No! I am a good girl," Maiko was saying.

"But you can't touch the artwork." That came from a tall, burly man in a guard's uniform. "That's not allowed. No touching, okay?"

"Okay," said Maiko, sniffling a little. "I did not know."

Mrs. Yashimoto rushed to them. She knelt down

to hug Maiko and spoke to her in Japanese. Then she stood up and faced the guard. "Sorry," she said. "Very, very sorry." She looked frightened.

"It's my fault," I said, joining them. "They're new here, and I didn't explain all the rules."

The guard nodded.

Mrs. Yashimoto still seemed upset. "It's all right," I told her. "Let's go sit down and I'll tell you what happened."

We headed out of the Rodin gallery and found a bench near some Impressionist paintings.

Trying to talk slowly, I explained to Mrs. Yashimoto that the guard was not really angry and that Maiko was not in trouble. Then I explained to Maiko that museums were places to look but not touch. She listened closely, nodding.

Finally, she jumped to her feet, all signs of her tears gone. "Can we go to the pool now?" she asked.

I checked my watch. "As a matter of fact," I said, "it's just about time to meet everyone there." We headed off for the Temple of Dendur.

It was a long, long day at the museum. As we drove home late that afternoon, I sighed with satisfaction, thinking of everything I'd seen in the past few hours. Gorgeous paintings. Silver swords with beautiful engravings. Egyptian statues and Chinese silks. Tapestries from Russia and furniture from castles in England. Going to the Metropolitan Museum of Art is like taking a tour through history *and* like going around the world, all in one day.

My feet hurt.

I was exhausted.

But I was happy too.

And when I thought about Stacey again, I knew just what I had to do. Spending so much time with the Yashimotos recently had made something very clear to me: Good communication may not be easy, but it's very, very important. Misunderstandings happen all the time, whether or not you're speaking the same language. And it's important to clear them up before they grow into something worse.

Like a fight between best friends.

It was time for me to talk to Stacey — for real. No more polite chitchat, no more angry words. Just straight talk. Maybe it wasn't too late to save our friendship.

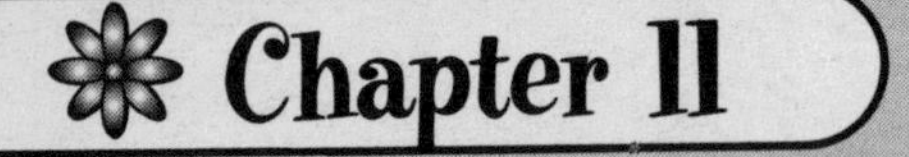

Chapter 11

I called Stacey as soon as I walked in the door that night; suddenly I couldn't wait to talk to her.

But Stacey's mom reminded me that Stacey was in New York for the weekend. (Can you believe it? We could have run into each other at the Met!) That meant that the earliest we could really talk would probably be on Monday afternoon, before our BSC meeting. I would have to be patient.

I saw Stacey on Monday morning as soon as I walked into school. Right away, before I could chicken out, I asked if she would come over early for the BSC meeting. "I think we need to talk," I said. She agreed without any hesitation. That made me feel good.

Stacey walked with me down the hall toward my locker, telling me a little about her weekend in New

York. Suddenly, she stopped short. "Whoa!" she said. "Check *that* out."

I followed her gaze. There, set against a bank of lockers, was a huge, bright bouquet of flowers. "Those are beautiful!" I said. "Look at those colors." This wasn't a wimpy bouquet with pink and white flowers. This was a powerhouse of color with red, yellow, purple, magenta, and orange flowers all bursting together.

We drew closer.

"They're by *your* locker," said Stacey. "That's funny."

We exchanged glances. She raised her eyebrows.

"There's a card on them," she pointed out. She bent closer. "Claud," she said, excited, "your name is on the card!"

"No way! Really? But who — " I reached down and picked up the card, my heart thudding a little. Had Jeremy finally decided to let me know how he felt? " 'Dear Claudia,' " I read. " 'Some flowers are red, some flowers are yellow, when I think of what you said, I feel like a lucky fellow.' "

"Who's it from?" Stacey asked.

There was no signature on the card. Just an initial. The initial "A."

"It's from Alan," I said, feeling a little strange.

On the one hand, the flowers were gorgeous, and I felt wonderful that someone cared enough to leave them at my locker. I was beginning to realize that Alan Gray could be a really sweet guy. On the other hand, I wondered if he was taking things a little too far. Was I going to have to have a talk with him? After all, I thought we were going to the dance as friends. Do friends send each other huge bouquets of flowers?

"Claud?" Stacey asked, examining my face. "Are you okay?"

I nodded.

"I'm impressed," she admitted. "I wouldn't have thought Alan had it in him. These are really nice flowers."

"But what am I going to do with them?" I asked. "I'd like to take them home, but I can't just leave them in the hall all day."

"You'll have to squeeze them into your locker," said Stacey. "I can't help you, though. The bell's about to ring and I have to go to my own locker. Talk to you later!" She took off down the hall, leaving me to figure out how to fit an entire garden into a tiny space that was already filled with gym clothes, notebooks, art supplies, and a few emergency items such as a Milky Way bar and a bag of Smartfood.

I did some quick rearranging. Then, just as I'd finally started to stuff the flowers into my locker, who should walk by but Jeremy. "Hi," I said. (That was about the most either of us had said to each other for at least a week.)

He didn't answer. In fact, he ignored me and kept on walking.

I gave the flowers one last shove, slammed my locker shut, and ran after him. "Jeremy," I called, "wait!"

He didn't even slow down.

I felt like a fool, but I kept following him. "Come on, Jeremy," I said.

He stopped and turned to look at me. His face was cold. "What do you want?" he asked.

"I — I just want to talk."

"I have the feeling you'd rather talk to Alan Gray," he said stiffly.

I looked at him. "What? Alan — ?"

"I heard you two are . . . you know."

It was then that I realized two things. First, Jeremy must have heard that Alan and I were going to the dance together. Second, he was hurt. Very hurt.

"But you don't understand," I said. "Alan and I are just friends. We're going to the dance, but that's because of this mix-up with a note I wrote for you. He got the note by mistake, and he thought it was for him, and I couldn't figure out how to tell him it wasn't, and — " I was babbling. Jeremy cut me off by raising his hand.

"That's your problem, not mine," he said.

"I'm sorry if — "

"Sorry for what?" he interrupted. "Forget it, Claudia." He turned and walked away.

I felt terrible. Somehow I'd managed to mess up everything with Jeremy. Not that it was totally my fault. After all, if he'd wanted to go to the dance with me, he could have asked. But I still felt bad. I could see how hurt he was. (Was I a little bit — just the teensiest bit — glad he was hurt? Maybe. Because maybe that meant he liked me.)

There didn't seem to be much I could do about it, though. Jeremy didn't want to talk to me, so I'd just have to wait until he cooled down.

Meanwhile, it was time for homeroom. I headed down the hall, my head spinning. How had things become so complicated? My life used to be simple. A best friend, my art, a Ring-Ding once in awhile. Then I had to go and fall for some guy. Now things were messed up with my best friend, and while I still had my art and plenty of junk food to console me, nothing was the same.

However, I had a feeling that Stacey and I were on our way to working things out. Once that was taken care of, maybe I could fix things up with Jeremy too. For now I was just going to have to forget about him.

I tried, but I didn't do a very good job of it. I spent most of my morning class time thinking about what to say to Jeremy. I forgot about Alan and the bouquet until he sneaked up behind me in the lunch line. "Did you like the flowers?" he asked shyly.

"I love them," I began, "but — "

"Wait," he said, holding up a hand. "Forget about that glop." He pointed at the tuna-noodle casserole on my tray. "Come with me."

"Come with you? Where?"

"Shhh," he said. "It's a surprise."

I looked down at my tray. I decided to take a chance. "Okay," I said, shrugging. "Lead the way."

We slipped out of the cafeteria, Alan in the lead. I followed him through the halls. He led me to the same empty classroom in which we'd talked when he told me how much he'd liked my note.

"After you," he said, bowing as he opened the door for me.

I walked inside, wondering what he was up to. I saw a flash of red in the far corner of the room. I looked closer and saw that two desks had been pushed together to make a table. A table covered with a red tablecloth — and set with silverware, nice china, and fancy glasses. In the middle of the table was a silver candlestick with a red candle in it.

"Lunch, madame?" Alan said, gesturing toward the table.

I didn't know what to say. "Alan, I — "

"Have a seat." He pulled out a chair for me. He lit the candle. Then he went to a counter at the back of the classroom and returned with a bottle of Sprite. "Champagne?" he asked.

I giggled. "Sure. Why not?" I held out my glass.

Alan filled it, then sat down and poured some soda into his own glass. "To the Cupid's Arrow Dance," he said. We clinked our glasses and drank. "Ahh. This was an excellent year for Sprite."

I laughed. I've heard my dad say the same thing about fine wines.

"And now for the first course," said Alan, jumping up. He went to the counter again and came back

with a bulging Burger King bag. "For you, madame," he said, pulling out a Whopper and fries. "And, of course, we have extra ketchup."

"Wow," I said, unwrapping the burger. "My favorite. And it's still hot. How did you pull this off?"

Alan shrugged, trying to look mysterious. "I have my ways," he said. I had a feeling he'd had some help from Cary Retlin.

I ate a fry. It was time to say something. "Alan, this is really sweet. I appreciate your effort, I do. And I loved the flowers. But you do know that we're just going to the dance as *friends*, right?" I gave him a serious look.

"I know," he said quickly. "Friends. I just thought we could get to know each other a little better. As *friends*. Or — whatever." He gave me a little grin.

I couldn't help smiling back.

This new, improved Alan could turn out to be a pretty interesting guy.

We ate our way through all the food Alan had brought, including a dessert course of Devil Dogs, Ho-Ho's, and Twinkies. We talked and laughed, and you know what? I had a very good time.

When the bell rang, Alan jumped up, blew out the candle, and started clearing everything away. I helped him fold the tablecloth and stow it and the silverware in his backpack.

"Alan," I said as we left the room together, "thanks. That was a lot of fun."

"Really? You liked it?" He smiled a big, goofy smile. "Cool!" He looked incredibly happy, as if he were floating on air.

"See you later, okay?"

He nodded. "Right. Later." He headed down the hall, looking dazed. I had to smile as I watched him walk away.

Suddenly, I felt somebody bump into me. Hard.

I turned to see Stephanie Boxer, a girl I knew slightly from when I'd been sent back to seventh grade. "Hi, Steph," I said.

"Ha," she said fiercely. "Don't play innocent with me. And stay away from Alan Gray. I've had a crush on him for a long time. He doesn't realize he likes me too — but it's only a matter of time. So hands off!" She didn't even wait for a reply. She just stormed off down the hall.

I stared after her. Someone had a crush on Alan Gray? Life was getting more complicated by the second.

Chapter 12

"Banana?" Mrs. Yashimoto's tone was unsure.

"Yes!" I cried. "Very good." It was Monday, after school, and I was tutoring Mrs. Yashimoto. We were working with a picture dictionary, a tool ESL tutors use a lot. It's a really cool book, full of pictures of everything you can imagine. There are pictures of toothbrushes and raincoats, cameras and Laundromats, violins and plumbers. There's a whole page about the post office and another about a restaurant, with every different item named: menu, waitress, fork, cashier.

One way you can use it is just to point to a picture and say the word so that the person you're tutoring can add it to his or her vocabulary. After all, most people have been to a restaurant before, even if it was in another country. So they know what a waitress is; they just don't know how to say the word in English.

Mrs. Yashimoto and I were working on a page that showed a grocery store and all its contents. She wanted to learn words for all the things she shopped for and used every day. We were working on the fruit section, and Mrs. Yashimoto was doing a great job remembering the words I'd already taught her.

"Peach," she said when I pointed at a picture. "Grapes."

The watermelon was harder for her. She paused when I pointed it out. "Juice fruit?" she asked finally.

I shook my head. "That's the right idea. It is a very juicy fruit. But it's a watermelon. Watermelon," I repeated.

"Watermelon," she said, smiling. "Good. Watermelon. I — I like watermelon."

"Excellent!" I exclaimed. Just then, Yoshi and Maiko ran to us, bored with the puzzle I'd given them to work on.

"I like watermelon too!" said Yoshi, squeezing in between us to look at the picture in the book.

"I like plums and oranges and grapes!" cried Maiko. "And strawberries. And — "

"You like fruit," I said, laughing. "I can tell."

Mrs. Yashimoto spoke to the children in

Japanese. I had the feeling she was telling them to go back to their puzzle.

"It's okay," I said, glancing at the clock on the wall. "I think our time is up anyway." I pointed to the clock. Mrs. Yashimoto nodded.

"Thank you, *sensei*," she said, bowing her head toward me.

Sensei is the Japanese word for teacher. "Thank *you*," I said, bowing back. "It was fun."

I was really enjoying our work together. And Mrs. Yashimoto had promised that as soon as she was better at English she would help me learn some Japanese. Hearing her talk to her children had made me think of my grandmother. I had started to think that learning to speak Japanese — at least a little — would be a way of honoring Mimi.

Later, as Erica (who had been working with the Bosnian family) and I walked home together, she told me she envied me. "You're so lucky to know about your heritage," she said. "I don't even know if I'm Scottish or Irish or Italian or what. If I could find my birth parents, I could learn more about my background."

"What if you found out you were a princess or something?" I asked, half joking.

"I used to fantasize about that," admitted Erica.

"When I first found out I was adopted, I used to think maybe my parents were famous movie stars or royalty. Now I know that's kind of silly. But I *would* like to know more about them."

I nodded. I used to love hearing Mimi tell stories about what life was like when she was a little girl in Japan.

"Plus," Erica went on, "I need to know about other things, like my family's medical history." She looked down at her feet. "I know, I know. You've heard this already. I just can't seem to stop thinking about it."

"That's okay," I said. "I understand. It's like there's this huge mystery out there. And even though you're happy with the life you have, the mystery still concerns you."

She nodded. "Thanks. It helps to be able to talk about it with you."

We had almost reached my house by then. I was a little nervous about The Talk with Stacey — nervous enough that I hadn't even told Erica about it. I checked my watch. "Oh, no," I muttered. "I'm late."

"Late for what?" asked Erica.

"I'll explain later," I promised, breaking into a trot. "See you!" I waved as I headed for home.

Stacey was waiting in my room for me. She was

sitting in the director's chair at my desk. "I let myself in," she said. "I hope that's okay."

"Of course it is." Stacey — and the rest of my BSC friends — let themselves into my house all the time. "I'm sorry I'm late."

"No problem. I've only been here for a couple of minutes."

We looked at each other.

"Well, I guess I'll put my stuff away," I said, slinging my backpack to the floor.

"Let me move out of your way." Stacey rose and stood in the middle of the room.

In the old days, Stacey would have thrown herself on my bed. She spent nearly as much time hanging out in my room as I did. But now we were doing this polite thing.

"You can sit on the bed," I pointed out.

"Oh, okay." Stacey perched on the bed. She looked like a person who was only going to stay for a minute, someone who didn't want to settle in.

I unzipped my backpack and took out the books and notebooks I'd brought home, stacking them on my desk. Then I took a seat in the director's chair. For a few moments, the room was quiet. I took a deep breath. The Talk had to begin somewhere.

"So, I thought — "

"What did you want to — "

Stacey and I started talking at the same time.

We stopped at the same time too.

The room was quiet again.

Then I started to giggle. I couldn't help it. Something about the situation just seemed so silly. Plus, I was nervous.

Stacey looked at me for a second. Then she started laughing too.

That seemed to break the ice. Once we got our giggles under control, I felt ready to talk.

"Look, Stacey," I said. "I just want to apologize for everything that's happened over the past few months. I'm not saying it's all my fault. But I am really sorry for my part. And I want us to be friends again. For real. I miss you."

Stacey looked down for a second. When she looked back up, I saw that her eyes were moist. "Claud, I miss you too," she said softly. "And I'm sorry too. Really sorry. I didn't mean all those horrible things I said."

Suddenly, it was as if I heard the echo of our voices. We'd had the worst fight of our lives right here in my room. Would we really be able to put it behind us? We'd called each other the most terrible names.

Brainless.

Stuck-up creep.

Liar.

Loser.

"I didn't mean the things I said either," I told her. "I really hate that we said them at all. Do you think we can forget them?"

She shrugged. "Maybe not. But we can put that time behind us and move on."

"Moving on sounds good." We smiled at each other — nervously at first, then for real. "And Stace? I think we should agree to something."

"What's that?"

"Let's never ever let a boy come between us again," I said.

"I swear." She raised her hand. "Never again."

I stood up and we high-fived. Then I tumbled down on the bed next to her.

"Claud?"

"What?"

"How come you're going to the dance with Alan Gray — instead of with Jeremy?"

I sat up. It was strange to hear Stacey say Jeremy's name so casually.

"If you don't want to tell me, that's okay," she said hastily.

"No, it's just — well, Jeremy didn't ask me."

She shook her head. "He must have been afraid you'd say no."

"What do you mean?" I asked. "Hold on." I reached beneath my bed and pulled out a giant-sized bag of peanut M&M's — and a bag of pretzels for Stacey. "Now that we're talking, I need some munchies."

Stacey took a pretzel. "I mean," she said, after she'd taken a bite, "that he broke up with me because of you."

I stared at her. "Really? You think so?"

She nodded. "I'm just about positive."

I looked down and noticed that M&M's actually *will* melt in your hand if you hold them in a tight fist long enough. I didn't know what to say. If Jeremy really liked me that changed everything. We could be going to the Cupid's Arrow Dance together! But I had already agreed to go with Alan, and it was too late to cancel on him now. Unless — for just a millisecond I let myself picture Stephanie Boxer, who would probably be thrilled to go with Alan in my place.

I shook my head.

It was time to talk to Jeremy and straighten things out for real.

Meanwhile, I thought, popping that handful of melted M&M's into my mouth, it sure was good to have my best friend back.

Chapter 13

Stace — Help! Jermy's avoyding me. Why do you think he wont talk to me? Chek one:

_____ He hats my outfit.
_____ He hats my guts.
_____ Heo' maldy in love with me but shy.
_____ Heo maldy in love with somebody else.
_____ He forgot who I am.

What shuld I do ??????????
anser fast. Im going nuts.
Claud

Claudia — Your note made me laugh out loud in math class and Wes (I mean Mr. Ellenburg) gave me a weird look. I know it's no laughing matter, but it was kind of funny to think Jeremy is avoiding you because he hates your outfit. Like boys even notice what we wear. Anyway, I didn't check off any of the choices, because I think it's something else. I think he's hurt. Really hurt. From what you told me, he's upset because you're going to the dance with Alan. Maybe you should consider changing your mind about that.

Stacey

S—

How can I chang my mind when Allan is being so SWEET? Even Kristy has to admit he's diffrent. Culd you believe todays present?

C

C—

Yesterday's was pretty good too. I see what you mean. Don't worry, we'll think of something.

S.

I stared down at Stacey's note. It gave me a great feeling to see her handwriting once again. We used to write dozens of notes a day, and I had missed that when we were fighting. Now, even when we didn't have classes together, we'd pass notes in the halls. We used to leave them in each other's lockers, but I had learned my lesson about that.

Still, even Stacey couldn't help me figure out my life these days. On the one hand, Jeremy was avoiding me. I barely saw him at all on Tuesday. On Wednesday he passed me in the hall twice, but both times he just waved without even smiling. He acted as if it would kill him to stop and talk. By Thursday morning I was going out of my mind. That's when the notes really started to fly between Stacey and me.

Alan, on the other hand, wouldn't leave me alone. Not that I minded, exactly. I loved getting so much attention. I don't know what it is, but a lot of times I go after boys who are more, I don't know, *unavailable*. Alan was the opposite. He was so available it was ridiculous.

Every day he told me I looked great and commented on some specific part of my outfit. "I love that vest," he'd say. "Did you really make the buttons yourself? Awesome."

And Stacey says boys don't notice what we wear.

He would smile at me in the halls, save me a seat

in study hall, buy me treats at lunchtime. "I know you like the kind with walnuts better," he said as he handed over a chocolate-chip cookie, "but this is all they had left."

He gave me presents too. Just little things, but they were carefully picked out. One day he brought me a magnet with a picture of a Michelangelo sculpture on it. Another day he gave me some charcoals. I knew he'd bought both at the art supply store I go to.

Alan was really being nice. And I can't explain it, but he did it without acting pushy or desperate or anything. He surprised us all with how *normal* he could act when he wanted to.

At lunch on Wednesday, even Kristy commented on it. "Alan has — changed," she said in a bewildered tone. Stacey and I had been talking about him, but I hadn't thought Kristy was listening. She seemed too busy poking at her "mystery meat," making faces as she tried to guess what animal it came from.

"He really has," I agreed. "I know it's hard to believe, but I think Alan Gray may finally be growing up."

"Ha," she said, putting down her fork. "We'll see about that. I'm not about to stop checking for whoopee cushions when I sit down near him."

"Fine," I said. "You do what you want. But I'm telling you, he's different." I had seen another side of Alan. A softer, romantic side. A side I had to admit I liked. Not that the old Alan was gone completely. Alan Gray was still a clown at heart. But I liked that too. He could always make me laugh just by pretending to slip in a puddle or by mimicking our principal.

On Wednesday afternoon, as I was leaving school, I ran into Cary Retlin.

"Hey, Claudia," he said. "Are you in a hurry?"

I shrugged. "Not really. What's up?"

He fell into step beside me. "I just wanted to talk to you about something," he began. "Actually, about Alan."

I paused. "What about him?"

Cary met my eyes. "He really likes you, you know."

I smiled. "I could kind of tell."

"I mean he *likes* you," Cary said without smiling back.

"Uh-huh." I stopped walking. "Cary, do you have a problem with that?" I asked.

He stopped too. "Not exactly. I just — well, Alan's a friend. A good friend. I don't want to see him get hurt."

"Who says I'm going to hurt him?" I felt a twinge of guilt when I remembered how I'd been tempted to break our date for the dance. I started walking again, and Cary followed me.

"I know you might not mean to." Cary was still looking very serious. "But let's face it, Claudia. He thinks that note was for him. I know it wasn't."

I drew a breath. "How do you know about the note?" Had Alan passed it all over school? I felt my face grow hot.

"He showed it to me," Cary said. "But just to me," he added hastily, seeing my look. "And I figured that you must have left it that day I opened his locker for you."

I felt a little better. "But how did you know it wasn't for him?"

Cary shrugged. "I just knew. I've seen how you look at that Jeremy guy. You never looked at Alan that way."

I had to admit that Cary was good at noticing things. But I was *not* about to admit that he was right. So I kept quiet.

"Anyway," Cary continued. "I can't help wondering why you're stringing him along."

I stared at him. "What's that supposed to mean?"

"It's an expression," he explained. "It means you're keeping his hopes up, even though you're not at all interested in him."

"I know what it means," I said, kicking a stone that appeared in my path. "But it's not what I'm doing. I like Alan, I really do. And I've been clear with him. He knows we're going to the dance as friends."

"He may know that," said Cary, "but it's not what he's hoping for."

I gulped. I knew Cary was right.

"He's trying really, really hard to convince you to see him as more than a friend," Cary went on.

I nodded. "I know that," I said softly.

"So please, just don't hurt him." Cary stopped walking, and I did too.

"That's the last thing I want to do," I told him. And I meant it.

"Good," said Cary. "That's all I wanted to know." He gave me a little salute. "Later, Claudia," he said. He turned and walked off quickly in the other direction, leaving me to stare after him.

Everything was changing so fast. First, Alan turned out to be a sweet, caring guy. Then Cary Retlin showed me *his* sensitive side. What was going to happen next?

By Thursday afternoon I was feeling worn out.

Alan had continued to give me all sorts of attention, and Jeremy had continued to avoid me. Cary gave me a Look every time he saw me in the hall. I was beginning to wish the dance were already over. Things were too complicated. At least I didn't think they could get worse.

I was wrong.

"Did you hear?" Stacey asked. She had stopped by my locker at the end of last period.

"Hear what?"

"Oh, you didn't," she said. "Oops. Well, it's not great news."

"What? Tell me!"

"Kristy told me that Mary Anne told her that she heard that Jeremy asked Emily Bernstein to the dance."

Thud. That was the sound of my heart hitting the floor.

Stacey gave me a sympathetic look. "I'm sorry, Claudia. I know he would rather have gone with you."

"Sure," I said, feeling dazed. Automatically, I put my math book into my backpack. "I guess that's it, then," I said.

"What do you mean?"

"There's no chance for me and Jeremy."

"You don't know that," Stacey said firmly. "You guys still haven't talked, have you?"

I shook my head.

"Then nothing's for sure. You need to talk to him."

She was right, and I knew it. So when I saw Jeremy in the hall as we were leaving school, I called to him.

"Hi," he answered. He didn't meet my eyes.

"I already heard that you asked Emily to the dance, in case you're wondering," I told him.

"So? What else should I have done? Wait for you to do something you don't want to do?" His face looked pinched.

I stared at him, shaking my head. "Forget it," I said. "Just forget it." I turned and walked away.

Chapter 14

"I, um, made it myself." Alan cleared his throat.

I stared down into the box he'd handed me. "It's really cute," I told him. "It" was a pin in the shape of a heart with an arrow through it. As far as I could tell, it was made out of Sculpey. The heart was a little on the lumpy side, and the arrow looked more like a fishhook. "I love it," I said.

And I meant it.

No boy had ever made me jewelry before. I felt a lump in my throat as I thought about Alan bent over a tiny piece of clay, working so hard to make something to give to me.

"You do?" Alan's face lit up. "Really?"

"Really," I said. I reached into the box and lifted the pin out carefully. Then I pinned it onto my dress in a spot where it would show up nicely.

It was Friday night and Alan had arrived to pick me up for the Cupid's Arrow Dance.

"You look awesome, Claudia." Alan was almost whispering as he gazed at me.

I had put a lot of thought into my outfit. (I know, what else is new, right?) The Cupid's Arrow Dance was not a dressy affair. But I wanted to look good. I had finally decided on a pink theme for Valentine's Day. But not frilly, little-girl pink. That wasn't me. I went with hot pink, paired with black to make it stand out even more.

I was wearing a short retro dress I'd found in a thrift shop. It had white trim and white heart-shaped buttons. I think it was from the sixties. I also wore clunky black shoes with a stacked heel and a square toe. I had a wristful of hot-pink bangles, and I'd pulled my hair back with a couple of pink barrettes.

"You don't think it's too much?" I asked him.

"Sure it's too much," Alan answered, grinning. "That's what's great about it."

"You look pretty good yourself," I told him. He had on a nice new pair of cargo pants, a cool pair of suede Converse All-Stars, and a big-but-not-baggy red shirt. Alan was not a bad-looking guy. Not bad at all.

My parents came into the front hall to see us off.

They've met Alan before, of course, since he's been around since we were both at Stoneybrook Elementary. Janine popped her head in too.

"You two look great together," she commented.

I noticed a blush creeping up Alan's cheeks.

"I mean, your color scheme matches," Janine said quickly. "Pink and red. Perfect for the occasion."

"Have a wonderful time," my mom said.

"But don't be too late," my dad added.

Alan and I exchanged glances. "We won't," I said.

Then Alan held out his arm and asked, "Shall we?"

I put my arm through his, and we marched out the door.

As Mr. Gray drove us to SMS, I thought about what I was doing. If you had told me a month ago that I would be going to a dance with Alan Gray, I would have said you were out of your mind. And now I was not only going with him, but I wasn't even embarrassed about it. I had begun to discover that Alan was a really nice guy. I didn't care what anybody else thought.

I love the moment of arriving at a school dance. It's always so exciting to approach SMS in the dark, see the light flood out of the building. It's the same place, only different. I spend hours there every day, but when I come back for a dance it feels as though I'm going to a whole new place.

Usually, I'm one of the people who decorates the gym for dances. But this time I'd been too busy with the Yashimotos, so I had no idea what the decorating committee had come up with and it was especially fun to enter the gym and be surprised by the balloons and streamers that changed the look of the room.

The DJ had already cranked up the music by the time we arrived, and lots of kids were there. Not many of them were dancing yet; it takes awhile for everyone to feel comfortable.

I glanced around the room, looking for my friends.

And looking for Jeremy.

I had to admit it. I had come to the dance with Alan, but Jeremy was still on my mind. What would he be wearing? Would he ask me to dance?

I saw Mary Anne and Kristy, who had arrived together. Mary Anne looked a tiny bit uncomfortable, since she's still not used to coming to dances without Logan. Kristy looked uncomfortable too. She never looks relaxed when she's dressed up.

I caught Kristy's eye and waved to her, and she

nudged Mary Anne and pointed me out. Both of them waved back.

Stacey wasn't at the dance. She had decided to spend another weekend in New York with her dad instead. I had a feeling she might have a date with Ethan.

"Want some punch?" Alan had leaned over to talk into my ear. The music was pounding too loudly for regular conversation.

"Sure," I yelled back.

He headed toward the refreshment table.

I watched him go, noticing how everyone who saw him pass smiled and waved. Alan might have had a reputation for being obnoxious, but he was also — in a weird way — sort of popular. Everybody knew him, and everybody thought he was a funny guy.

I felt someone bump into me from behind, and turned around. Stephanie Boxer was glaring at me. She was wearing a flouncy white dress, dripping with lace. She looked just a teeny bit like a bride.

"I can't believe you're leading him on like this," she hissed. "How could you let him think you actually like him?"

"I *do* like him," I said, putting my hands on my hips. "And why is it your business?"

"Because I *love* him," she said, narrowing her eyes. "And I don't want to see him get hurt."

I held up both hands. "Wait a second. Nobody's going to get hurt."

Just then, Alan returned carrying two cups of punch. Stephanie gazed at him for a second, then melted into the crowd.

"What did — ?" he started to say.

I waved a hand. "She's just — never mind." I shook my head.

Alan handed me my punch, and we stood sipping and watching the dancers. The DJ was picking up the tempo by then, and more kids were on the dance floor. I scanned the crowd — and then I saw him.

Jeremy.

He was dancing with Emily.

I felt my heart do a little flip. Then I looked at them more carefully. I don't know how to explain it, but there are things you can tell about people by the way they dance together. Serious couples dance one way, people who are interested in each other dance a different way. And friends? They're easy to spot too.

Jeremy and Emily were definitely dancing as friends, not as a couple.

I let out a sigh of relief.

Alan glanced my way. He couldn't have heard my

sigh — the music was way too loud — but I had the feeling he knew what I was thinking.

"Want to dance?" he asked.

"I — " I didn't know what to say. I didn't feel ready to dance yet. "Why don't you ask her?" I suggested, pointing to Stephanie. She was standing nearby, making an effort to look anywhere but at Alan and me.

Alan looked at her, then back at me. "I'd rather wait to dance with you," he said. "Just let me know when you're ready."

I smiled at him. He was being all sweet again. The DJ cued up one of my favorite songs. "Okay, I'm ready," I said to Alan. "Let's go."

We danced to three songs in a row. Alan had a good sense of rhythm. I was surprised. He seemed comfortable on the dance floor.

"How did you learn how to dance like that?" I yelled over the music.

"Watching MTV," he yelled back. "I just copy whatever they do. It's fun!"

I started copying his moves. We were moving to the beat as if we'd been dancing together all our lives. I was having a great time.

"Mind if I cut in?"

Alan froze in midstep and stared at — Jeremy.

"Um, no," he said. "That's okay. I mean, if Claudia wants to — "

Jeremy looked at me. "Do you?" he asked.

Those eyes. That smile. How could I resist?

"Okay," I said.

Alan nodded and disappeared.

And then it was just Jeremy and me.

The song Alan and I had been dancing to ended and another one began. A slow one.

Jeremy and I looked at each other for a moment. Then he held out his arms and I moved closer. We started to dance, swaying together to the beat.

"You look great," Jeremy said into my ear.

I felt my heart beat a little faster. This was the moment I'd been waiting for and wondering about. Were we finally going to tell each other the truth about how we felt?

If we were, I had to figure out what I was going to say.

I liked Jeremy. But did I *like* like him?

Maybe not. And maybe I didn't care so much if he liked *me* that way.

Maybe we were meant to be "just friends," after all. Because that's how we were dancing. Even though we were dancing to a slow song, we were dancing like people who are friends. We weren't holding close, or looking into each other's eyes. Anyone who was watching would have known in an instant that we were buds. No more, no less. Just friends.

I realized something else just then too.

I realized I would rather be dancing with Alan.

Which made absolutely no sense.

No sense at all.

Chapter 15

I moved closer to Jeremy and closed my eyes. I rested my cheek on his shoulder and took a deep breath, taking in the fresh, clean scent of the shampoo he must have used only hours earlier.

Jeremy, I said to myself. *You're dancing with Jeremy. Isn't this what you wanted all along?*

I was trying to convince myself that it was so, but it just wasn't working. Sure, his hair smelled good. It looked good too. I still thought Jeremy was one of the cutest guys around. But something was missing. I should have been thrilled to be dancing with him — and I wasn't.

I wasn't exactly miserable about it either. Jeremy was a good dancer, and he was a good friend. I didn't mind spending some time with him. But —

"Claud?" Jeremy had stopped dancing. He stepped away from me and gave me a curious look. "Something's wrong, isn't it?"

"Well . . ." For a second, I considered denying it. But I could see by the look in Jeremy's eyes that he already knew. I glanced down at my feet. Then I met his eyes again and nodded.

He gave me a crooked smile. "I guess we were doomed from the start," he said, shrugging.

I frowned. "Doomed?" We had moved out of the center of the dance floor by then and were standing in a quieter corner of the gym.

"Maybe that's too strong a word," admitted Jeremy. "But you know what I mean. It seems like we just weren't meant to be a couple."

I nodded slowly. Images passed through my mind: I remembered again the first time I saw Jeremy and that I'd liked him right away. Then I thought of seeing him with Stacey — in the halls, at a movie. I remembered how much that had hurt. I pictured Stacey and me fighting over Jeremy. Stacey. My best friend! I'd almost lost her over this guy. I gave my head a shake and smiled at Jeremy. "I think I understand," I told him.

"It's like we started out on the wrong foot,"

Jeremy said. "That mess with you and Stacey and me. I think it ended things before they could even begin between us."

I nodded thoughtfully.

"I did some things wrong," Jeremy went on, looking into my eyes. "I know that. But now I want to start over."

What did he mean? Was he still thinking we could be boyfriend and girlfriend?

"I just want us to be friends," Jeremy said, as if he'd read my mind. "I want us all to be able to talk to each other: you, me, and Stacey. I like you both too much to lose you as friends."

"You won't lose me," I said. "We can definitely be friends." Jeremy really was a cool guy. I was impressed, but I still wasn't feeling that old tingle.

We smiled at each other.

Jeremy reached out and pulled down a pink balloon that was hanging nearby. "Here," he said, "this goes with your outfit."

I laughed and took the balloon. He helped me tie the string around my wrist.

"So, friend," he said. "Want to dance to one more song?"

"Sure," I answered. "Just for old times' sake."

We walked back onto the dance floor. A fast song

was playing, so we didn't dance close. But I *felt* close to Jeremy. He and I understood each other in a new way.

We danced until the song ended, making up silly steps that made us — and everybody around us — crack up. When the song ended, Jeremy gave me a big hug. "Later," he whispered into my ear.

"Later," I replied.

Then I left him to find Alan.

I scanned the dance floor, but didn't see him. I checked out the refreshment table, but he wasn't there either. Kristy and Mary Anne were hanging out, drinking punch.

"So you and Jeremy looked like you were having a good time," Mary Anne commented.

"We were," I told her, still scanning the gym. "But it's not what you think."

"Who are you looking for?" Kristy asked curiously.

I paused. Then I looked her right in the eye. "Alan," I said. "I'm looking for Alan."

She took a breath and started to say something, but I saw Mary Anne shoot her a Look.

"He's over there," Mary Anne said, pointing toward a spot near the bleachers. "With Cary."

I saw him, and guess what! My heart did that little flip thing. The thing it used to do when I saw Jeremy.

That was interesting.

"I bet they're making fun of everybody," said Kristy. "I can just imagine what they have to say about that tie Mr. Kingbridge is wearing."

I hadn't seen the tie yet, but Kristy was probably right. Making fun of people was Alan and Cary's favorite thing to do.

But as I walked toward them, I saw that they seemed to be having a serious talk. Neither of them noticed me until I was right next to them. I tapped Alan on the shoulder. "Hi," I said.

He turned — and when he saw me, his whole face changed. His eyes lit up, and he gave me a huge smile. "Claudia!" he exclaimed.

Then he looked around. "Where's — where's Jeremy?" he asked.

I shrugged. "I think he's dancing with Emily."

Alan gave me a curious look. "And that's okay with you?" he asked carefully.

"Totally. Totally and completely okay."

The smile reappeared. "Cool," said Alan. "Cool."

Cary gave him a little shove.

"Um, so, do you want to dance?" Alan asked.

The DJ had just put on another slow song, a really romantic one. The lights were low in the gym by then, and lots of couples were on the floor, swaying to the music.

"Yes," I said. "I'd love to."

Alan led me onto the floor. Then he put his arms around me and we began to move to the beat.

I could feel people staring at us. And I knew what they were thinking: "Claudia and Alan *Gray*? Is she crazy?"

Maybe I was.

But I didn't care.

L. GODWIN

Ann M. Martin

About the Author

ANN MATTHEWS MARTIN was born on August 12, 1955. She grew up in Princeton, NJ, with her parents and her younger sister, Jane.

Although Ann used to be a teacher and then an editor of children's books, she's now a full-time writer. She gets ideas for her books from many different places. Some are based on personal experiences. Others are based on childhood memories and feelings. Many are written about contemporary problems or events.

All of Ann's characters, even the members of the Baby-sitters Club, are made up. (So is Stoneybrook.) But many of her characters are based on real people. Sometimes Ann names her characters after people she knows; other times she chooses names she likes.

In addition to the Baby-sitters Club books, Ann Martin has written many other books for children. Her favorite is *Ten Kids, No Pets* because she loves big families and she loves animals. Her favorite BSC book is *Kristy's Big Day.* (Kristy is her favorite baby-sitter.)

Ann M. Martin now lives in New York with her cats, Gussie, Woody, and Willy, and her dog, Sadie. Her hobbies are reading, sewing, and needlework — especially making clothes for children.

Baby-sitters Club Friends Forever

Look for #8

MARY ANNE'S REVENGE

I dropped my pack on the floor and sat down. I pulled a ballot box toward me — and realized that Cokie was in the room too. She came out from one of the computer stations and said, "You're late, Mary Anne."

I felt Abby's scrutiny. My neutral expression hadn't been as neutral as I'd thought. Clearly some of my misery was showing on my face.

Cokie saw it too. I swear I saw her eyes light up. "Are you all right, Mary Anne?" she asked with fake concern.

"I'm fine, thank you." My hands fluttered uselessly among the slips of paper.

"You certainly don't look it," Cokie purred. "You look *awful*."

Suddenly, I couldn't take it anymore. I felt my eyes blaze with rage. I stood up and faced Cokie. "Well, it takes one to know one, doesn't it, Cokie.

And you of all people ought to know about awful, because in my opinion, when they were handing out awful, you were first in line."

Cokie actually took a step back.

Austin scooted his chair a little away from the table, as if he were afraid we were going to start throwing things.

Abby said, "Mary Anne?"

Without another word, Cokie whirled around and stomped out of the office.

Austin said, "Wow, Mary Anne. You don't hear someone talking like that to Cokie every day."

"No," I said. I was shaking. I'd stood up for myself. Literally. I sat down again.

"Impressive," said Abby. "I'd say you just won a major battle. Wait till I tell everyone that Mary Anne Spier silenced Cokie Mason. Way to go!"

"Thank you," I said.

I'd won the battle. But I wasn't too sure about the war. Cokie would strike back. I was sure of that.

But this time I'd be prepared.

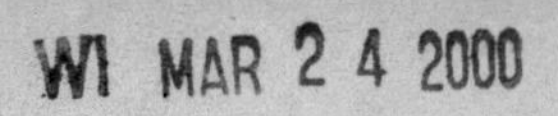